The Ugly Post

A love story

The Ugly Post

A love story

SAILOR PENNIMAN

DARROW PUBLISHING | LOS ANGELES

Los Angeles, California

A Darrow Publishing — Equality book

Published in the United States by Darrow Publishing.

ISBN 978-0-9993487-0-3

1 2 3 4 5 6 7 8 9 10

www.darrowpublishing-losangeles.com

For

Seven Letters

Contents

One

harlie panicked. He recognized the obvious screen name: **BryceIsMyScreenName**. It belonged to the man Charlie had lived with for seven years. Bryce hated screen names and had long before come up with one he could easily remember, which revealed little about himself. He used it all over the Internet to gain entry to places, but usually that was it. Charlie had never known him to join the melee that was Internet opinionating. There the name was, though, squatting at the top of the comments section, surrounded by words presumably written by Bryce, below a post titled "Straight Cop, Gay Love" on a blog Charlie had never heard of.

It was Monday. Charlie had arrived home ahead of Bryce and logged onto the desktop computer they shared. In the browser history, he saw an unfamiliar Web page. Bryce had obviously gone there. Charlie, naturally, went there too. It was a gay men's lifestyle site, more magazine than message board. Charlie had been relieved for that.

Then he noticed "Straight Cop, Gay Love". The link to it was the only one on the page that was a clicked-on red. Every other link was an untouched teal.

Charlie wondered why his partner was interested in gay straight cops, apparently enough to be the first to comment about them. He could have read Bryce's post to discover the answer, but he was on edge. He wasn't sure what he'd find. Instead, he hurried through the article looking for answers.

Nothing jumped out. A straight man had fallen for a gay one. The twist implied in the title—that the man was a cop—was no twist at all. He was just a straight man torn between his wife and a gay friend he'd developed feelings for.

Charlie wasn't sure what to make of the author. He loved two people, one of them more than the other, the one he hadn't expected to love. He fretted about what to tell family. He debated whether he should convince people he wasn't bi or gay, just in love, but thought doing that would send a bad message. Charlie agreed. The man chose instead to identify as gay in honor of the love of his life, for whom he had left his wife. He desired a relationship filled with intimacy and affection between his lover and him but bemoaned that it was hard to engage in sex because he wasn't enticed by his partner, although he did enjoy kissing him. Charlie was uncomfortable. The cop included details he could have spared the reader about specific techniques he hadn't grasped and how he had used gay porn to learn how to make love to a man. He was caught between the splendors of gay romance and not being able to naturally express them. *Where did Bryce fit into that equation?*

Charlie glanced at Bryce's comments again, without reading them. A couple of paragraphs, three replies. He had probably said what Charlie had already thought himself.

Charlie didn't have much time. Bryce would be home soon.

He read Bryce's post.

The benign-looking blocks of text turned out to be a fast-moving, malignant cancer, which traveled through the lymphatic system of Charlie and Bryce's relationship and killed it by the time Charlie read to the end of what **BryceIsMyScreenName** had written:

> Great post. Hang in there on the attraction thing. I know what I'm talking about. I've been with the same person for seven years. We're both 34. I'm gay. He's gay. But he's not what I would call "all of that", whereas I've never had any problems in that area. I'm not naturally attracted to him, but I'm okay with it. I love him and can definitely say that what he lacks on the outside doesn't even seem missing. The relationship is the best. And all the rest, if you know what I mean, is great. Happily monogamous here. It came down to looking past what isn't there to know how lucky I am. You'll get there.
>
> It sounds like you love Michael. Speaking from experience, you just have to say, hey, I love this person, so, hey, I can't care that they're not

> my type or that there are other people out there I
> could be with or who I'd more obviously match
> up with, who travel around in a category I'm
> more used to. Love is love. It conquers all,
> including an attraction mishap. There's a reason
> you're together. My relationship is proof that you
> have to look at obstacles relative to the rest of
> what you have. If they matter, you'll know.
> Luck to you and Michael. Thanks for sharing
> your story.

With that, Bryce announced to the world something he had never told Charlie: He had spent their entire relationship unattracted to Charlie. The cop's story about not being enticed by his lover had triggered a sympathetic response from Bryce and drawn him out. Bryce seemed to be commiserating, as though Bryce found Charlie as unappealing and uninviting as the cop did his boyfriend and needed to relate to someone about it. He had spent more words talking about himself and Charlie than about the cop and his partner.

There was something worse. The cop had seemed thrilled to rearrange his life for his lover, sexual foibles between them, and all, and had been almost apologetic for deficiencies Charlie didn't even see as shortcomings. He worked hard to tear down barriers between himself and his partner, taking the blame for some of the kinks. Bryce sounded as though Charlie had been unworthy of him and as though Bryce had made serious sacrifices and gone to great lengths to do Charlie the favor of ignoring his failings and his below-average countenance, one that had no chance of measuring up to Bryce's, so they could be together. He made no mention of any difficulties Charlie may have had in accepting him. At least the cop had turned to the Internet to try to find ways to measure up. Bryce assumed there was nothing he could do to cure whatever was lacking between him and Charlie—except suck it up and "hang in there", as he told the cop to do—because it was all Charlie's fault. The replies to Bryce's post shattered Charlie.

STILLGOTVINYL said:

That must have been tough, Bryce, getting together with someone ugly and working past it to find something good, when you've got it going on, and knowing that everywhere you go, people probably wonder how you ended up together. Seven years. Wow.

APAULOGIZE said:

Vinyl, I don't think Bryce said his boyfriend was ugly, but, yeah, it would be hard to be with someone all that time if they weren't cute, especially if you're on the hotter side, and you know you're missing out on what else is out there. All the possibilities. Dudes checking you out and you have to act like you don't see it and like you don't want to tap that. I couldn't do it. Nights would be rough, y'all. Precisely why monogamy is B-A-D. It's better to taste a little of everything. If your partner isn't much to look at, it's not as harsh.

STILLGOTVINYL said:

Paul, Bryce went out of his way to post about not being attracted to his partner. That's code for ugly, even if he himself doesn't realize it. He doesn't say how they met, but however they hooked up, like dude here leaving his wife for a guy, he probably had feelings before he knew what hit him, and there he was, a hottie with a hideous boyfriend, trying to make it work. It happens. Not trying to be mean. Go back and read. Bryce brought it up. And, disagree. Monogamy is G-O-O-D. That's why you shouldn't pick someone who doesn't really do it for you.

It ended there. There were no rebuttal posts by Bryce insisting he wasn't a hottie with a hideous boyfriend or that Charlie *did* do it for him. Apaulogize had no comeback either. Still Got Vinyl had apparently made a convincing case. The humiliation flattened Charlie.

His cell phone lit up with Bryce's face. The frame was all striking eyes and gorgeous hair. Charlie stared at the image, which usually caused anyone who saw it to remark, "Is that your boyfriend? Damn, he's cute." He barely read the text that came with the picture. *Got food. Home in a few.* Charlie turned the phone face down without replying. Wherever Bryce was, Charlie was suddenly embarrassed to have Bryce's phone light up with *his* face.

He logged off the computer in a daze. He thought about how he and Bryce became a couple. Still Got Vinyl had been right. They met by accident in a weekend motorcycle class that ended with a DMV license test on Sunday afternoon at the course site. During breaks, Charlie and Bryce sometimes migrated toward one another—a journey that was easy for Charlie; Bryce was arresting. Hyperbole and comparisons to the Greek god of beauty Adonis were fitting for Bryce, especially when one considered that Adonis was a rough translation of the word "lord". Bryce had command of every second he walked around in. He sported the image of a carefree, dark-haired Santa Monican who had gone to high school on a beach and majored in volleyball in college, but he was an assertive, erudite romantic, who didn't know how to spell Grindr, let alone use it. He had never needed to learn. Charlie had held his own, though, alien to meet-up apps for a different reason. He was okay with solitary life, even if he wasn't content. Until something unfolded that changed his status as a single man, he had been prepared to accept the way of things and would nip at no one's heels while he waited.

He kept his own counsel that weekend. He and Bryce had had an early moment in which they stared hard at each other. There was no question for either of them that the other was gay, but Charlie made no obvious moves. When he and Bryce met in the middle, it seemed to be a coincidence. It turned out, they got on brilliantly, each self-assured for different reasons.

They passed their DMV tests and celebrated together. They texted constantly over the following week and went to a big-screen revival of *Vertigo* that Friday, as their official first date. The same night, they fell into bed because the way of things had changed, and they had fallen in love. They had been there ever since, in bed on a regular basis and in love all the time.

Monogamy had also turned out to be the way of things, happily for Charlie. He had thought for Bryce, too. It had seemed easy. Their love had around it a kind of fortress built from its depth and strength, which guarded their union well. It kept them safe. Others had no way in. They made sure of it.

Charlie reflected on their years together. His mind was drawn to their time in bed. He had figured what happened there had been an extension of what went on outside the bedroom. After seven years, he and Bryce still flirted and laughed and courted. At night, they brought that to bed and had a fabulous time. They were buttoned down in regular life, but in bed, there were no boundaries, no set roles. Everything was possible, and they proved it endlessly with uninhibited sex play and exploration of fantasies. The plane of their bed was directionless and limitless, with no head or foot or implicit guidelines for positions. There were heavy doses of romantic propositions, too. They kissed each other sometimes for hours at a stretch and carried on conversations in bed with their mouths touching the whole time. Their relationship was closed and not open, and they tried to be for each other all of what else was out there. Charlie had thought they had succeeded. He never proclaimed to be as drop-dead dazzling as Bryce, but he assumed that once Bryce loved him, he naturally found him sexually attractive.

Bryce made it clear in his comments that Charlie was wrong, that what they had was false. It had to have been, when Charlie considered what Bryce had written. The physical and the emotional didn't blend for Bryce as Charlie figured they blended for all people in love. Even Charlie saw Bryce as a different version of handsome once he had fallen in love with him. Proximity had changed the shape of things and had made Charlie's impressions of Bryce unique and special and wrapped up in how he felt about Bryce. Bryce was no longer a beautiful stranger with no meaning in his face who fell into a neutral, impersonal category of attractiveness. Who he was inside changed the definition for Charlie of what he was outside.

But sex and love apparently diverged for Bryce. Who Charlie was failed to transform him for Bryce into a body which seemed one way to Bryce and another to everyone else, and which transcended superficial judgments and placed Charlie outside the reach of petty assessments. As Bryce had urged the cop to do with his gay lover, he had muddled through and choked down the sex for the sake of the intimacy. He probably loved Charlie despite himself more than because of Charlie.

Or *did* he love Charlie? Charlie had just glimpsed good-looking people offering condolences for substandard partners, a conversation he wouldn't be privy to if he hadn't bumped into it. After what he read, he questioned it all and wondered how Bryce could have made such a laughingstock out of a man he claimed to love. Bryce had sounded different, so free and as though he was among his own, in his advice to the cop. *How often had Bryce discussed Charlie behind his back and told him one thing and said another to presumably beautiful people who would get it, like the sexy cop? Maybe Bryce envied the cop's gay lover, Michael, and wanted to be Michael and show the cop how to love a man the right way, the way Charlie couldn't. Who* was *Bryce?*

Charlie was destroyed. He broke down. It was the first time he had cried in years.

He knew what he had to do.

He would leave Bryce and deliver him from the trap he had been caught in seven years earlier. He had no choice. He didn't see how he could continue to live with a man who had lied, with an impostor who wasn't attracted to him.

———◦◦◦———

Bryce walked in the door ten minutes later with a crisp paper bag full of hot Chinese food. Charlie had just stopped crying. He was self-conscious. He wanted to hide his face. Had Bryce thought he was ugly always, even just standing in the kitchen?

Bryce leaned in for his "I'm home" kiss, but Charlie shied away. Were even their casual kisses rough on Bryce, as Apaulogize had suggested? Charlie was suddenly jealous of the cop's boyfriend, Michael. At least his partner enjoyed kissing him.

"What's wrong?" Bryce said.

"Nothing. I think I'm catching something. Don't want you to get it." There was a nugget of truth in the fib. He felt so grotesque, he naturally wanted to keep Bryce from being exposed to it. It was the first lie Charlie had ever told Bryce, a small one to contend with Bryce's big one. It didn't matter. Soon, Charlie would be gone.

"Uh-uh," Bryce said. "Come here." He kissed Charlie square on the mouth. "I guess we'll be sick together." He stuck close to Charlie.

Normally, Charlie loved it that Bryce's sense of boundaries where he was concerned was off-kilter. Bryce always stood or sat or lay or slept "too close". With everyone else, he maintained the proper distance, but when it came to Charlie, he lost all perspective. He gave Charlie just enough elbow room to make a sandwich or turn the pages of his book or run his razor over his face and no more. Their bed had a footboard as tall as its headboard. Bryce had chosen that bed expressly for lazy weekends when they lounged around in it with pillows piled high and read. It let them lie in opposite directions, which gave Bryce access to Charlie's feet and the ability to reach out and lightly stroke them when he felt the urge. Bryce's love of proximity had always enchanted Charlie. That evening, though, for the first time, it made him uneasy. He wondered how much of it compensated for a lack of sexual attraction to Charlie.

"If you're sick, why aren't you in bed? Your eyes look red, almost like you've been crying." He brushed Charlie's cheek with a light touch and stole another kiss. "Go. Take the trays, and I'll bring in dinner." His smile was affectionate and flirtatious and warm. He behaved as though nothing mattered while Charlie was sick except making sure Charlie was comfortable. He turned a laser-like focus on serving Charlie his dinner.

Maybe I'm wrong, Charlie thought. And then he recalled the words "not all of that" and "missing out" and "category" and "hideous" and "ugly" and "Seven years. Wow." and others that made him cringe and knew he wasn't.

"That's okay. I can eat out here."

"I know, Babe, but you shouldn't. Go. I'm right behind you. No rice, though. Gets in the sheets."

Charlie tormented himself. Was it love he received or politeness or habit or the hard work of faking it that Bryce disguised well? Charlie wished it were half an hour earlier, when he hadn't even known to ask the question.

Moments later, Charlie found himself in the awkward position of being fed dinner in bed by a man he planned to leave. He stared at Bryce's granite jaw, smooth skin, and green eyes, which always seemed greener under Bryce's dark hair, and considered his own plain face, boring hair, and unremarkable countenance. Charlie's best attribute was his perfect weight. It gave him a nice butt and a well-defined body that carried an average-sized head, which wore short, average, white-guy hair that was no style. He had no stand-out bad features such as a unibrow or crooked teeth, but, other than his ass, a cut-looking waist which made him seem twenty-five with his shirt off, and a decent pair of hairless calves, what he did have wasn't arranged in any kind of alluring way. At least, he didn't think so. Bryce was right. He wasn't "all of that", just some of it.

He felt retroactively embarrassed for the previous seven years of exposure, of nudity, of presumed equality that wasn't there, of unabashed assumption of status Bryce secretly never thought he had a right to claim. He wanted all those years back, all those moments he flirted and strutted and demanded attention when angry, as though he mattered, and made love with abandon and behaved like he didn't need to be self-conscious when, all along, he should have been.

He felt conspicuous and exaggeratedly ugly with the truth exposed. He was humiliated beyond what he could stand. He was devastated by the deception and mortified to think it could have continued, with him oblivious, if he hadn't discovered Bryce's secret. He could have been Bryce's permanent fool.

He ate sweet-and-sour shrimp and was demolished.

Two

"*I know* something's wrong," Bryce said.

They were in bed with the lights off. Bryce lay as close to Charlie as possible without touching him. Charlie kept his back to Bryce and sent vibes that told Bryce he shouldn't come any nearer. They formed an awkward spoon.

It was Wednesday, two nights after Charlie had found Bryce's post. Charlie hadn't spoken much since he had read Bryce's words. Bryce still had no idea Charlie had seen what he had written.

Charlie had begun the process of leaving. It made him wistful and polite but only enough unlike himself to worry Bryce without giving him anything to fight against. Charlie continued the "getting sick" fib to keep his distance. It wore thin, though, especially as he still went to work every day. His credibility had only one thing going for it: Bryce's autopilot was set to TRUST, as Charlie's had once been, until Bryce's public advice to the cop had thrown off Charlie's instruments and forced him to navigate the rough patches without the safety of the benefit of the doubt.

But Bryce also began to question the clouds on the horizon. Charlie figured he finally suspected they were headed for heavy turbulence. Charlie didn't think Bryce knew, yet, though, that they were about to crash into the side of a mountain and crack up into tiny pieces which wouldn't be put back together.

"Why do you say something's wrong?" Charlie said.

"Because I just know. I love you. I know when something's wrong. And something's wrong. You're barely speaking to me, which is just weird. I don't know why you won't talk to me."

Charlie's stomach did a little lovesick flip as Bryce's tender words traveled on his warm breath down Charlie's bare back to the waistband of his boxer briefs. Charlie gave in a little and tried to sound natural. "I *am* working through something, Babe, I can't lie," except he did with his next words. "No need to worry."

"Should I be scared?"

Charlie could tell he already was. "No." Another lie, for the short term. In the long run, Bryce had nothing to fear. He would be better off. "I promise I'm not angry or cheating or quitting my job, or anything. I just need a little time." Truths, about not cheating or quitting his job, surrounding what may or may not have been a lie. Charlie wasn't angry. He was well beyond anger. He seethed. He was bitter and resentful and terribly hurt, feelings that were far less fleeting and less potentially transient than anger and which symbolized great hurdles, permanent objects in their way.

The duplicity and dishonesty in Bryce's attitude about their relationship were insurmountable for Charlie. Bryce had reserved a private space for himself where only he understood all of what was between them because only he had known the truth. That was indefensible, as Charlie saw it. He felt patronized and humiliated. Bryce had told the cop to look at obstacles relative to the rest of what was there and had warned that if they mattered, a person would know. Charlie took Bryce's advice and looked at the obstacles his feelings presented, and he knew that they mattered and that they would never not matter.

"Okay," Bryce said.

An hour later, Bryce sent more warm air down Charlie's back. "I know you're awake."

"I never pretended to be asleep." After a long while, Charlie said, "Did you ever notice?"

"Notice what?" The question came slow, almost as though Bryce hadn't wanted to ask it.

"That my name's Charlie and yours is Bryce?"

"You never noticed that your name's Charlie and mine's Bryce?"

"No."

"Babe, what's wrong?"

"Nothing. Good night."

Bryce seemed to have surrendered to his own needs. Or maybe he felt more pity for Charlie. He inched close to Charlie and put his arm around him. "My mind's racing with everything you're not saying."

Did he know? "What is it telling you?"

"I don't want to speak the words out loud. I'll wait until you're ready. But we'll get through it, you know? Whatever it is."

We won't.

Bryce gave Charlie an extra squeeze and grazed his neck with a kiss. As much as Charlie hated to indulge himself, he took advantage of the obscurity the blackness lent his physique and edged back a tad, against the comforting feel of Bryce's bare skin, relieved that his best attribute—his tight, well-shaped behind—was what nestled against Bryce. The way they lay there felt to Charlie like a metaphor for what their relationship had been: Two men in love who worked better in the dark.

Charlie didn't care just then. He settled into Bryce's spoon. Bryce planted several quick kisses in the soft space between Charlie's shoulder blades and let his mouth rest at the base of Charlie's neck. His steady flow of warm breath trapped between their bodies soothed Charlie's back. Bryce gently caressed Charlie's feet with his own. He eased into a calming cadence which enveloped Charlie's feet and told Charlie with each gentle stroke that Bryce wouldn't abandon Charlie, that he wouldn't take his feet away, that he held on, emotionally, as much with his feet as with his arms and his heart. Charlie was lulled into a relaxed bliss. He was in love.

And he loathed himself for succumbing. He had no pride.

——•◦•——

Charlie spent two more days in a haze. It was Friday. It was the last time he would fake sick. It let him lag a little in pretending to leave for work and hide from Bryce that he had taken the day off. It meant a little more face-to-face exposure than Charlie preferred, but he put it to good use. He asked Bryce to take the following Monday and Tuesday off.

"Why?"

"I'll explain tonight." Charlie planned to leave that night. Even though Charlie felt Bryce would be happier with Charlie gone, seven years *was* a long time. The news, at least initially, would blindside Bryce. Charlie wanted him to have more than the weekend to recover.

"All right," Bryce said. "Does this mean you're done working through whatever it was and we're gonna have some fun?" He only half-smiled. He stood farther away than usual.

Charlie closed the gap. "You are finally going to have the fun you deserve," Charlie said. Standing so close to the man he loved with everything in him, he surprised himself, after days of resentment and aloofness and timidity about his looks, and leaned in for a kiss. He realized it was probably the last kiss he would ever share with Bryce. He lingered and added nuance to it. He was saying goodbye. He felt the sting behind his closed eyes that came with the onset of tears. He held his lids shut and prolonged the kiss to stave off crying. The longer it went on, though, the more difficult it was not to break down.

Bryce returned the kiss with relief more than passion. "Babe," was all he said, but Charlie knew he meant, *Thank goodness. I thought I had been permanently banished.* Charlie felt awful since, just nine hours later, he would be.

Bryce's tired smile gained a little cheer. He didn't try to advance his position. He left for work while he was finally a sliver ahead.

Once Bryce was gone, Charlie rode his motorcycle to his new place. He had found a small apartment in Culver City, a landlocked section of Los Angeles that was geographically schizophrenic. It lay east of Santa Monica, where Charlie and Bryce lived, and jutted up against the east side of the most hated thoroughfare in America, the 405 Freeway, Los Angeles's north-south aorta, but it was still on the city's west side, close to Marina Del Rey, just south of Century City and Beverly Hills, without the beach life the Marina offered or the elegance of the nooks to the north. The apartment had been available right away, so Charlie had taken it.

After Charlie deposited his motorcycle, he caught a private taxi service back to his car in Santa Monica and headed out to buy two trunk-sized suitcases. On the way to the store, he stopped at the bank and moved exactly fifty percent of his and Bryce's shared savings into his own, single checking account.

He returned to Santa Monica with the trunks at ten-thirty. For half an hour, he stood paralyzed in the living room, unsure what to do. Finally, he moved some clothes into one of the cases, and by that small action, started the clock on the beginning of the end.

He wept for hours as he moved things from all over their home into the luggage. They had rented the house in a corner of Santa Monica which was far from the Promenade, the mall, and the heavy foot traffic fanning out from the pier. They had each tried to be an excellent wage-earner for the household. It made them ambitious ladder-climbers with serious seniority at their jobs. A by-product of that success was that, over time, they had outfitted their home with fine furniture and little luxury items which put the finishing touches on every room. It had taken years of effort and, at times, had been grudging in its pace, with water-heater, tree-stump, and roof-repair setbacks along the way, but their house had become a snug haven and a showplace.

A condition of their lease was an option to buy at the ten-year mark, with many concessions made by the seller based on certain obligations, including those tough repairs, having been met by Charlie and Bryce during the rental period. They were just three years away. They already planned and saved for a huge housewarming event that would include flying in favorite cousins and college roommates and, in Bryce's case, his host family from when he had been an exchange student in France, as a high school junior. It was going to be an extravagant beach-and-Los-Angeles bash. Charlie had even suspected Bryce planned to ask Charlie to marry him and to turn the celebration into a wedding party. Charlie's answer would have been yes.

It devastated Charlie to reduce their lives into two suitcases from Target. He would leave most of it behind. He wanted almost none of it. It no longer symbolized what he thought it had. He would take only his personal items and a few treasures he couldn't live without. If he had to fight Bryce for them, he'd do it.

It was a strange endeavor. He took some things because they reminded him of Bryce and rejected others for the same reason.

He tried to get hold of himself. When he left Bryce later that night, he would need to keep his composure. The last thing he hoped would happen when storming out on a lover he repulsed was "the ugly cry".

Charlie's phone lit up all day with Bryce's face.

Charlie never sent his face back to Bryce.

Three

Bryce came home annoyed. "So, you *are* alive."

"Yes."

"Would you mind telling me why you ignored me all day and why you didn't tell me this morning that you won't be at work *for the next two weeks*?"

"I—"

"I called you at work and got, 'I will be out of the office until....' What the hell, Charlie? Maybe it's just me, but I thought something like a two-week absence from life was worthy of a conversation."

Charlie thought it ironic Bryce reproached him about discourse that should occur between them.

"Too bad I found out it *was* just me," Bryce said. He was in rant mode. Charlie would let it play itself out. It would be better that way.

"And don't tell me you didn't know I was calling your cell. Do you have any idea how scared I was something happened when you never answered, especially when I didn't see your bike in the garage, just now? I thought you and it were splattered somewhere." He spotted the suitcases in the living room. "What the—? Are we going somewhere? What is going *on*?"

Charlie resisted the instinct to check Bryce's parental tone or bother with explanations. None of it mattered. "No."

"No? What does, 'No,' mean?"

"No, we're not going anywhere."

"Well, then what's going on?" He slowed down and looked at Charlie. "Oh, no. Are you sick? Your eyes are red again." He touched Charlie's forehead.

Charlie felt grotesque with his face so close to Bryce's.

"Feels cool." While Bryce was there, he gave Charlie an unsure version of his "I'm home" kiss. Charlie almost recoiled, for Bryce's sake.

Bryce lost a little of his bravado. "You don't look good, Babe. I'm sorry for getting on you. I just—"

"It's okay. I'm fine."

Some of Bryce's nerve returned. He echoed Charlie with a deadpan, faux-bored tone. " ' I'm fine. I'm working through something. I look sick. I'm not. I left an hour early three mornings in a row, to avoid Bryce, and then stayed home and hid the fact that I'm taking two weeks off.' I can't take much more of this, Charlie." He sounded irritated, but he looked petrified.

Charlie handed Bryce a packet of stapled together sheets of paper. It was a printout of Bryce's post and the replies. Several straggler comments had appeared. The count was up to sixty-three, all but one in agreement with Still Got Vinyl. Charlie's only ally had been **TeaLeaves**, who thought Bryce was full of himself. Otherwise, much to Charlie's humiliation, the debate about how revolting he was raged on in cyberspace. He was the measuring stick for body odor, bad bathroom habits, moles, dank breath, crusty knees, carpenter's crack, rolls of fat, big ears, zits, ugly feet, and back hair.

"You won't have to take any more of it. I'm leaving. For good. Because of that." He had envisioned he would be self-righteous in that moment, his big moment, that he would declare stand-on-the-table victory, but he was woeful and eager to escape.

Bryce gave the top page a cursory read. His eyes widened. "Where did you get this?"

"Isn't it obvious? You posted it. Well, you're free, now, no longer trapped in a relationship with a hideous boyfriend." He headed for his luggage. Bryce followed him. "With two suitcases, I won't be able to dramatically storm out. It's gonna be two, slow, embarrassing trips to the car." He grabbed the first trunk by its long handle.

"Put that down. What is this?"

"I told you." Charlie tried to wheel around Bryce with the suitcase, but Bryce got in his face. Bryce tended to be diplomatic when they disagreed, but Charlie had never ignored him all day and openly hidden things from him and lied to his face.

Bryce was confrontational. "You're leaving," he said. It was more statement than question, more incredulity than outrage. "Over a stupid Internet post." Another statement, a rude one and unlike him. He waved the printout. "Is *this* what all of this has been about?" He uttered a short, shocked laugh. "I literally thought you were dying. I thought you were *dying*, Charlie."

He almost sounded like he thought Charlie *should* be dying just to compensate for Bryce's shock that he wasn't.

"I was scared to say it," Bryce said. "I didn't want to speak it into being." He was disbelieving. "It turns out, you're pissed about a *reply to a blog post*?" He let out another burst of surprised, mirthless laughter.

"Yes." Charlie realized Bryce didn't take him seriously. Bryce thought Charlie was grandstanding to make a point. He was feeling confident and ready to put Charlie in his place and end the nonsense once and for all, not just that day's nonsense, but the entire gloomy week of fretting over what he deemed to be something unimportant, maybe even a waste of his energy. He seemed irritated by all the upset but also looked relieved, as though all matters had been cleared up and they could get back to the business of being a carefree couple as soon as Charlie came to his senses and maybe even apologized for causing strife.

Charlie hung onto the suitcase. Bryce would soon get it that he was leaving. The way Charlie saw it, his choices weren't limited to happy or dying. Some miserable space in between qualified him to be righteous in his pain.

He couldn't stand the sight of the thick printout flapping in Bryce's hand and snatched it. "You can't expect me to stay when I know you've faked it all these years. Repulsed. Grossed out. Feeling stuck." He tried again to sidestep Bryce, but Bryce grabbed his shoulders.

"What are you talking about?"

Charlie was suddenly incensed and sick of hiding and of being self-conscious. He was fed-up with feeling guilty for wearing his own face, the only one he had, and with *being* guilty of the unavoidable crime of walking around inside his own body and victimizing Bryce with an ugly boyfriend. He was tired of the lies. He erupted. "I'm talking about you telling the world you're not into me! I'm talking about those people arguing over whether I'm ugly or hideous and how rough nights are for you with me and you saying nothing to the contrary to shut them up! I'm outta here! You're free. Free to find someone who's 'all of that'. Goodbye, Bryce."

The speech had a little problem. Bryce still held onto Charlie's shoulders. Charlie was unable to punctuate his tirade with a smooth walk out the door.

"What the *hell*? This is crazy! And I never faked it with you one day in my life!"

"That's a flat-out lie." Charlie yanked himself free. Finally, he stepped around Bryce and dragged the suitcase away.

Bryce tugged on one of his arms and spun him around. Charlie dropped the suitcase handle.

Bryce grabbed Charlie's shoulders again and gave him a little shake. Charlie knew it wasn't violence. It was an attempt to get Charlie to see reason. The tone of Bryce's voice dropped and carried a gloomy warning. "Charlie, this isn't funny. It's downright dangerous. Don't say things that will push us somewhere we don't want to go."

"We're already there!"

How could Bryce be so obtuse, Charlie wondered, especially after he'd seen his own devastating words on the page and the others they had spawned?

"And you're telling *me* it isn't funny? You're warning *me* about *words*? *I know it isn't funny!*" Then the thing Charlie dreaded and which he swore he'd avoid at any cost occurred. He started to cry. He accepted it, but he would do whatever it took to forestall the ugly cry.

"Charlie, Babe, hang on, I'm sor—"

"*It's the worst thing I ever heard in my life!* My partner told the *whole fucking Internet* that he's not attracted to me! That I'm not all that! That I lack things on the outside!" His tone turned bitter. "That he had to get past our attraction *mishap*." Tears dripped off his chin, but he didn't sob. His face was serene. "He stood by—or sat by the computer—and watched while people called me ugly and hideous and compared me to the worst they had ever been with. Scabby knees and zits and crusty feet."

The anger kept the tears in check. He went with it. "I wonder, do you have to picture I'm somebody else when we're in bed, with my face close to yours, or do you just pretend I'm not there and think of me as a kind of inanimate sex toy so you can get off? Yeah, I'm sure nights *are* rough. What do you do to block out this," he waved his hands up and down his body in the tiny space between them, nicking Bryce's face with the printout, "so you can get through sex with me? I'm not your type? Well, go find somebody else! We are over! You'll never have to touch me again! Let go of me!"

Bryce was aghast.

He released Charlie's shoulders in slow-motion. "*Oh, my God.* Give me that thing again." He reached for the printout.

"So you can frame it?"

"Give it to me!"

Charlie handed over the pages.

Bryce read the top sheet of paper closely, the one with his post and the first few replies. When his eyes landed on Still Got Vinyl's initial blast, the packet shook in his hand. The pages rattled as he turned them, one by one, and read the abuses toward Charlie and the invective that had broken out among the commenters, people who were convinced Charlie, and foul lovers like him, who killed the happiness of those stuck with them, were dogmeat—a word used—and who wouldn't go down without a good stab at a blazing retort, all at Charlie's expense. Halfway through the long string of insults, Bryce closed his eyes. "Oh, dear God." The first signs of terror entered his tone. He looked right at Charlie. "This isn't how it sounds. This is out of context."

"Bullshit. It's *right in* context." He brought his palms together with a philosophical, professorial air and aimed them downward at the printout. "It's *right there*. Everybody got it. They all knew just what you meant."

"No, they didn't!" Bryce was desperate. "I never even saw these comments! I posted and logged off and never went back!"

Charlie had already figured as much, but it was too late for him. He saw that realization come over Bryce's face. Bryce understood what he had wrought and the damage he had done. "Does it even matter?" Charlie said. "In a way, it's worse. You made it clear. They all figured it out and came to the same obvious conclusions without any more help from you."

"They figured out nothing!" Bryce was frantic. He threw the printout on the floor. "They figured out nothing!"

"Then tell me what they missed!" He still cried.

Bryce talked fast. "All I meant was that when we met, you weren't really my type, but it turned out it didn't matter because I wanted to be with you. I love you." He grabbed Charlie's shoulders again. "I love you! You know that. How can you doubt me?"

"Because behind my back," he said, as he sniffed, "I'm not— *present-tense*—'all of that', according to you. Code for 'ugly', according to Still Got Vinyl. And sixty-something others! I had to find out by walking in on you talking about it with any asshole with an Internet connection!" It was Charlie's turn to be incredulous. "Why did you even bother with me? *For seven years*, you let me believe in…so much that wasn't true. You're a liar, and you let me expose myself. Do you know how unfair and selfish that is? And entitled! How can I *not* doubt you? And do you hear yourself? You just admitted it! 'You weren't my type, but it didn't matter.' Well, it matters to me!"

"Are you saying I don't love you, that I somehow used you?" He dropped his arms from Charlie's shoulders. His voice shook with fear and tears that loomed somewhere not too far behind his eyes. Charlie could almost hear them rushing forward from where he stood. They would reveal themselves before long. Charlie couldn't let himself care. Nothing had changed or would ever change.

"No. It's much worse. I know you love me. I've figured that out these past few days."

"Exactly! Which is why I said the relationship is the best and that everything was great. Did you read that part?"

"I did. That doesn't mean you're not in purgatory, like that cop, who told the whole world *his* lover was a turnoff, *good God*, his poor boyfriend." He snorted with disdain. "You're stuck with a man you love but who you settled for, who's not what you want, who you talk about and humiliate behind his back because, deep down, you don't think he's worthy of your respect or of *you*. And you've lied horribly, *for years*, to cover it up."

The tears broke through and poured out quickly. The difference was, Bryce was beautiful when he cried. His already gorgeous eyes became larger, more appealing versions of themselves with the tears magnifying them. His efforts to control his emotions only made his jawline appear stronger. He was handsomer than ever.

"I've never lied about loving you or about anything else. Ever. I respect you deeply, more than any human being alive. You are precisely what I want." His voice was full of despair. "You *have* been since the first time I saw you. Half the time, I wish I *were* you."

"Even though it's ugly over here?"

Bryce was stunned. He had a confused, hurt air made more striking by the emotion and the tears. It intoxicated Charlie and almost drugged him into forgetting his own pain.

"My words were indelicate," Bryce pleaded. "I only meant that sometimes a person can be perfect for you because they *don't* fall into that arrogant stereotype of being plastic and empty. A person can be wonderful to look at and to stare at in the kitchen or in bed, and not be a supermodel."

The drug wore off just enough to bring Charlie back to his senses. "Like you? Who's 'never had any problems in that area'?" He made air quotes.

"God, that's not what I mean. I mean he can be genuine and smart and funny and friendly and the easiest person to be around. Your best friend, Charlie. Your protector, your soul mate. Don't you get it?"

"No."

"You're beautiful because of the way you are. I was trying to tell that cop not to worry if the man he loved didn't fit his usual type because someone different—not *defective* —could make him much happier, maybe even *because* he wasn't obvious."

"A fascinating toad?"

"Oh, Babe, no."

"I'm as different from what you want as a man is for that straight guy who fell in love with a dude he couldn't make love with. You read his problems, and the first thing that came to mind was me! You *thanked* him for sharing his story! Like it was some therapy you've been craving from a support group!"

The urgency returned to Bryce. "We came to mind, yes, okay, yes, but in terms of how much we love each other, even though, if we hadn't taken that class, we probably wouldn't be together! I wasn't saying you are the same kind of turnoff that a man would be for that straight guy. That cop wanted to be with the man he fell in love with! That was the point!"

"A special exception to an otherwise steadfast rule, so to speak? A lover who squeaked through and got in by default?" Charlie retrieved the pieces of paper and flipped back to the first page. "Not naturally attracted to him...what he lacks on the outside...looking past what isn't there...not my type...other people out there I could be with...who I'd more obviously match up with...an attraction mishap...obstacles."

"Please stop reading," Bryce said. He sounded wretched. "That's not how I meant any of that."

"I can't see how else you meant it. And I can't stay here. *Don't you see that I can't stay here?*"

"No, I don't see that! Stay. We'll work it out. Let me work it out. I don't want you to leave. Please don't leave, Charlie. This is crazy!"

"You think I want to leave? I have to." The ugly cry was just seconds away. Charlie swallowed hard to stanch the tears. He spoke in a measured tone. "You've kept this hidden for *seven years.* You see a difference between us. I can't be around you anymore." He had to stop talking or the ugly cry would be the next thing that happened.

"I can't believe you can say that to me."

Charlie hung onto thin air. "I can't believe what you said *about* me. And I can't spend the rest of my life leaving an hour early every day so you won't see me coming out of the shower." He was done and done in. The humiliation was complete.

"Oh, no." Bryce sounded emotionally destitute, as though Charlie had robbed bare the cupboards of his soul and left him with empty shelves of rotted wood that would hold nothing. His face said, "What have I done?"

"I'm going now." If Bryce let Charlie leave, without either of them saying another word, Charlie thought he could get the suitcases into the car without breaking down.

Bryce was desperate, though. He stood right in front of Charlie. Charlie barely kept his composure. He didn't move.

"You were just sick," Bryce said. "A hotel is no place for someone not feeling well. Stay a few more days. Just please stay. Please."

Bryce stood close enough to reach up and wipe away Charlie's tears, which Charlie thought he might do. If that happened, the ugly cry was a foregone conclusion. "I wasn't sick." He dug into the explanation, as a distraction. "That night you came home with the Chinese food, I had just read this." He waved the pages. "I was self-conscious about being around you. I didn't want you to kiss me." He found courage he didn't think was there and looked at Bryce. "The thing about being sick just popped into my head. I *had* been crying, like you accidentally guessed."

"Oh, Babe." Bryce's face was full of pain.

Charlie dropped the printout. He was exhausted. He had to leave.

Bryce grabbed Charlie's hands and held them gently but firmly in his.

It was torture for Charlie.

"We can get past this once we get past the anger."

"No, Bryce." Charlie nudged the packet with his shoe. "We'll never get past that." He looked down and, even through tears that blurred his vision, could just make out the words "hideous boyfriend" on the top page. He had read them a thousand times. His eyes knew exactly where to find them.

He pulled his hands free and picked up the suitcase.

"Where are you going?" Bryce sounded bone tired, shocked, defeated in a game he had had no time to prepare for, a game whose rules he learned as he lost at it.

"I found a place in Culver City." More business. It helped.

"Culver City?"

"I know. It was the quickest thing available."

"Are you moving in with somebody? My God, Charlie."

"No."

It was strange, but Bryce cried a little more and looked more beautiful for it. "You don't have to do this."

"I do. You'll be happier in the long run. You'll see."

"I'm happy now, with you."

"Because it's all you know."

"It's all I want to know. It's all I've ever needed to know." His voice was leaden. Loss had begun to settle in. "I don't see how you could believe anything else. I love you. I love you." He looked at Charlie with attractive, tear-filled eyes and slayed him. Charlie almost put his suitcase down and gave in to Bryce's pleas. At that moment, he didn't want to leave.

"If you knew how often I was jealous," Bryce said, "how I've tried to grab hold of you and hang on, how far away you sometimes seem, even when you're right there, because I love you so much and can't get close enough, you wouldn't strand me like this. It's cruel, Charlie."

Charlie was frozen. He was unsure what to do. He was torn between the Bryce who stood there and begged him to stay and the one who posted those horrid words that hatched so many others. He remembered Bryce had spent seven years telling him one thing when he meant another. He had his answer.

He worked his way to the foyer. Bryce straggled along at a distance.

"I moved my half of the savings account into my checking account," Charlie said.

Bryce gasped.

"I left you three months' rent on the table," Charlie said. "Post-dated checks, but cash them whenever you like."

Bryce looked bewildered. "And after three months? Are you coming back?"

"No. I figure by then, somebody will have turned your head and moved in. We moved in after just four weeks. That tiny apartment." Charlie wished he hadn't brought up how happy they had been in those first weeks. He had almost made it out without losing all composure, and he was on tenterhooks again. He tried to talk his way out of the bind he'd just put himself in. "That place was so small," he said. "I still can't believe I had to convince you to leave it for this place."

"It was cozy. I loved it. I could have lived there with you forever. I moved here because it was where you were," Bryce said.

"It turned out all right." Charlie took a heavy, wobbly breath. "The beginning of...."

"A lifetime," Bryce said. "When I came to live with you, I wasn't pining for the love of my life. I was moving in with him. Four weeks felt normal. It was exciting. We were together all the time anyway. This is very different, Charlie. Can't you see that?"

Charlie shook his head.

"How can you leave everything we've built here? We're so close to having everything we want. Look around you. You're walking out on all of it?"

"I took what mattered most. You can keep the rest. I don't want it anymore." Charlie was gutted.

Bryce swayed a little where he stood. Charlie thought his knees might buckle. "Babe, I can't take this massacre. Have I broken us so completely that your love is gone? Have my words made you think you're that replaceable for me? Am I that easily replaced for you?" With that, Bryce lost it. He cried freely and desperately, without shame.

Charlie was jealous of Bryce, not because he could cry with abandon and suffer no embarrassment, but because he was unattainable. And brave. He had muddled through for years with a man who turned him off. There was a nobility in that, even with the lies. Charlie admired Bryce immeasurably and loved him more. "No, Bryce. I imagine I'll be alone a long, long while. In fact, as you get over us, please don't be angry, or at least don't lash out. I told you, I don't want things to be this way. They just are. I expect to be quite miserable. You won't be adding anything if you unleash on me."

Bryce sobbed. "I could never do that to you."

Charlie nodded. "Okay."

"And I will never get over you. Don't say that. Babe, this is insane. It's not real."

It was very real.

Bryce looked destroyed. "What if I want to talk to you or see you?" He barely choked out the words.

Charlie pushed on through his own tears. "The address is with the rent. But I don't want to see you or talk to you for a while. Not for two weeks, at least. Please."

"*Two weeks?*"

"Yes."

"I see."

Bryce said no more, but Charlie guessed he wanted to say, *Two weeks away from work, two weeks away from me. You've arranged that nicely for yourself.* Finally, Bryce said, "You're upset. You shouldn't be driving. Please. Will you stay overnight? You can still leave in the morning."

Charlie needed several moments before he could answer. His heart broke for Bryce, bargaining away his tomorrow and telling Charlie he could go if only he'd stay one more night. "I need to leave tonight. I'll be fine."

Bryce's face was soaked with tears. "Will you at least text me when you get where you're going?"

All Charlie could do was nod. He opened the door. "I'll be back for the other case in a second," he managed to say.

A few minutes later, Charlie had both cases in his car. Bryce sobbed the entire time.

Charlie returned to the foyer and placed his house keys on the antique stand near the door. "Those are yours." Fresh hot tears poured down his face. "Goodbye, Bryce." He made no sound. His face was still. He had made it through without ugly crying.

"Charlie, I'm sorry. I'm so sorry. I love you."

Charlie wished Bryce wouldn't say another word.

Bryce didn't grant Charlie's wish. "I'm going to find a way to make this right," Bryce said, speaking the words in strained half-syllables.

"I don't see how you can," Charlie said. "Besides, you're better off without me." He looked away. "I'm better off without you."

He was gone.

———◆———

I made it, Charlie texted when he had both suitcases inside his new home.

I love you, Bryce texted.

I love you, Bryce texted again.

Four

I t was Saturday. Charlie expected the maintenance guy to stop by and show him where he could mount a wall unit. It had been two weeks and one day since Charlie had set Bryce free, and he told himself he had to do something, anything, to establish that he had a new life, as dismal as it was.

He barely used his apartment, and it had gathered dust. He tidied and sang all morning a song he had set to repeat to get him through the mindless chores. He had a nice voice Bryce had always admired. He imagined Bryce was there, listening.

He showered and dressed and turned off the music. It had been a tad too loud for a looming visit from a landlord's spy. He examined himself in the mirror. It was the first time his face wasn't swollen and red and wet since he had moved to Culver City.

He had cried most of the time he had been away from Bryce. He cried in his tiny bedroom, on his rented couch, and in fetal position all over the standard tan carpet. The previous night he had finally won a small battle and forced himself not to weep so he could face the maintenance guy without a puffy face. He looked better for the reprieve, but he missed the crying. He would be back at it as soon as he was alone. He only had two more days before he returned to work and before he would have to stop crying completely. He needed to get in as much as he could while he had the chance.

There was a knock at the door. Charlie was glad the maintenance man was early. The sooner they finished, the sooner Charlie could strip down to a T-shirt and underwear and return to the floor and to his sobbing.

Charlie opened the door, and his heart dropped.

"I figured it might be okay to knock, since you stopped singing," Bryce said. He sounded nervous. "I got here a while ago. I've been out here, listening." He looked drained. His face had taken a beating like the one Charlie's had, only worse. He had cried more recently, maybe even right outside the door that morning.

It didn't matter.

He was striking.

"I'm sorry to come over without calling."

Charlie couldn't speak.

"Last night made two weeks."

Charlie said nothing.

"I've been home that entire time waiting for today. May I come in?" His eyes pleaded. He made no pretense at pride.

A full minute passed, during which all Charlie thought of were Still Got Vinyl's slurs. *Ugly. Hideous.* Charlie had almost worked past those affronts and all the name-calling and moved beyond what Still Got Vinyl and Apaulogize and Energee Lights and the rest thought of him. The ability for individual smears to sear through him had faded a tad. He relied a little less on Tea Leaves calling Bryce arrogant as a salve for his wounds. Over the most recent days, he had experienced generic pain and trauma, which hovered like fog and felt like a portent of a dark future. The magnitude of missing Bryce and the permanence of it had finally edged out most of the rest. Bryce standing at his door hurtled all sixty, plus, offenses to the front of his mind, each one stabbing him the way it had when he first encountered it.

Charlie considered closing the door without saying a word.

Instead, Charlie moved aside and let Bryce into his strange new world. He shut the door and found his voice. He heard himself ask a bizarre question, when he considered he asked it of the grand love of his life standing in an alien place his lover's betrayal had driven him to. "You've been off for two weeks? That can't have gone over well with Juliet."

"What did you think? That I would use that Monday and Tuesday you arranged for me to run a few errands and slide into work on Wednesday and clear voice mails and talk baseball? And Juliet was fine. Fine enough, anyway. I squeezed in the do-or-die to keep her off my back. My cell phone saved me."

In the darkened hall, Bryce had looked worn-out. Beautiful but tired. In the apartment, with light reflecting off the undecorated white walls, he looked grim. His voice was grainy and stretched thin. Charlie could see, then, that his eyelashes were wet.

"I don't know what I thought would happen," Charlie said.

"I can tell you. You emptied my life. And you have me worried about you over here in this apartment, by yourself, believing I don't care about you. That's absurd, Charlie. All I can think about is you and how hurt you are and how I can make it up to you and fix it all. I wish you would come home and let me take care of you."

Charlie wanted to give in to Bryce's sympathy, to fall into relationship mode and let Bryce, who did love him and who would know what Charlie needed, tend to his wounded soul. But Charlie remembered all the years he bared himself to a man who found him unsightly and lied about it. Any tenderness would be interwoven with a similar deception and cause the same shame. Charlie was done intermingling love and lies. "I'm fine."

"Are you?"

He knew Bryce wanted him to say yes…and no. He said nothing.

"I gave you your two weeks because it was the least I could do after wounding you so badly with that ugly post."

"Pun intended?" Charlie felt ashamed as soon as he said it. He had already left Bryce. He had nothing to gain by being nasty.

Bryce ignored Charlie's comment. "I confess I drove by here every day. And parked. And waited in my car for hours for you to come out, but you never did."

Bryce had parked outside of his apartment?

"After four days of that, I gave up and went back to just driving by, except for one other time, when you still didn't come out."

The settling apartment walls creaked in the stone silence.

Bryce kept talking. "You have no idea how good it feels to finally be standing here looking at you."

"You parked outside? Of here?"

"Yes. You sound surprised. It should be obvious. We've been together seven years. I never expected us to end or to be away from each other. It's unnatural not to be wherever you are. At least, to me it is. I wanted…."

Charlie waited, but Bryce offered no more. "You look tired," Charlie said and immediately wondered why his entire side of the conversation was plagued with inane non sequiturs.

"You're stating the obvious again. Of course, I look tired. I spent the first hour you were gone standing in the same spot where you left me. I've been in shock ever since. I don't sleep. I barely eat. I feel like shit for what I did, and I'm angry with you for I—." He sighed. "Never mind."

"You can say it. Leaving. And I can see you're about to lay into me even though I told you I'm already miserable." He finally made sense, but he hated their conversation.

"That's not what I was going to say. I was going to say, 'lying.' I've been doing a lot of thinking, and it occurs to me that you are the one who lied all these years."

Charlie was the liar? He wished he could cancel the maintenance man. "Me? How so?"

"You've always promised to trust me, but as soon as my feelings were tested, you gave me no benefit of the doubt. You drew your own conclusions. You lied about trusting me."

Charlie's face was granite. "So, you came over here to tell me other ways I suck?"

"What? No—"

Bryce had flipped on the switch to Charlie's rage. Charlie choked on his words. "You cashed in on my trust. On the Internet." He barely controlled his temper. He raised his voice. "You put it on blast that you're better than I'll ever be. And I heard you. Along with everybody else." He felt the need to shout. "You are gorgeous! I am a frog! I'm revolting!"

"You're not revolting!" Bryce yelled. He was stressed and disoriented. He dipped as quickly as he had peaked. "I'm sorry. I'm sorry. I swore before I came over here that I was just gonna be happy to see you and not screw it up, but, once again, I'm an idiot. I'm the asshole. I've made it worse, if that's even possible. I don't know what's wrong with me. Please," he said.

He paced up and down Charlie's small living room. To Charlie, he seemed like a junkie begging for a free fix from a heartless dealer who wanted up-front cash. "I came to ask you to come home. I thought maybe I had a leg to stand on, some bargaining power, and I've blown it. But cut me some slack! I didn't mean those words the way you heard them. Why, *why* is that so hard for you to believe?" He sounded more junkie-like, talking to Charlie and to no one in particular, gesturing at the air in the room and attempting to convince the withholding dealer with logic. "Do you think I would take pleasure in ridiculing you with *anyone* behind your back, that the last seven years were a lie? If you do, then, yes, as much as I risk pissing you off, I wonder what we had." It was akin to the junkie's final desperate tactic, to appear the disappointed customer who may take his business elsewhere, even though he was bankrupt and was begging *that* dealer because he had no options, except Charlie knew that unlike the junkie, Bryce meant his words, even if Charlie was full of doubt. It was a sad conversation.

"It's hard for me to believe a lot of things," Charlie said, "especially that we loved each other, considering." Charlie's explosion of a few moments before had turned into a dud. He was gloomy again.

"Loved?" Bryce's pacing stopped dead.

"I can't believe we managed it somehow, knowing, as the world also now knows, that I failed in so many areas."

"*Fucking Internet,*" Bryce said. "And this is what I'm talking about. You still haven't *asked* me how I feel. You think you already know. You won't hear reason." He was about to pace again, but Charlie rested a hand on his shoulder.

It felt wonderful to touch Bryce again.

He hadn't expected Bryce to show up, but once he was there, Charlie needed him as though he had begged him to come.

Bryce heaved a huge sigh. "You won't listen. You stay gone. You've stayed gone this entire time. You talk about our love in past tense. You look refreshed. You seem happy to be done with me and to be away from me. I'd guess I've shed a million tears to your few." He spoke to Charlie as a sad child would talk to an adult who had put their foot down.

"There's where you're wrong." All immediate anger and strangeness had faded. Charlie moved his hand and touched

Bryce's cheek. It was heaven. He pushed aside doubts about his looks and indulged a desire to regard Bryce for as long as the unexpected moment would permit. "Right where you're standing, I've lain cramped and miserable, for hours, choked by tears and torn up by how much I miss you. I'm trapped in a cul-de-sac, Bryce. I want to return to what we had, but I hit a dead end at your words, and I circle back out again. I see no solution."

Bryce leaned in a little. It was the most natural thing on earth for them.

Charlie's resolve disappeared. He kissed Bryce.

Bryce kissed him back with abject desperation. "Babe, yes. Please. Yes," he said.

They exchanged tender kisses, with prolonged pauses in between them that let them ponder each other and prepare to relish the next one. The spaces were filled with sexually charged glances, moments they usually would have used to take the temperature on the early play and assess whether the kisses hit their marks and whether each had tempted the other to want the next logical thing—lovemaking.

A surreal haze of glorious exhaustion and thrill settled over Charlie. The unexpected gift of getting to kiss Bryce when he thought they'd never again touch one another overwhelmed him. He knew they should stop, but they worked into an irresistible kiss-glance-kiss-glance pattern, which took on a life of its own, almost as if following the beat of a metronome set to its slowest speed.

Kiss.

Glance.

Kiss.

Glance.

Kiss.

Charlie broke away. "We can't."

"Why not? What more proof do you need that I want you?"

"You love me and maybe even want some part of me, the part of me you love—"

"Part of you? I love all of you, Charlie."

Charlie kept talking, as though Bryce hadn't spoken, "—but I can't forget what you said. A person can like what they have and secretly want more."

"I don't feel that way, Charlie. Please."

"You feel 'good enough'. But that's not...good enough. Something made you write that post. Go, Bryce. Find what you're looking for."

Charlie's words did not align with what he wanted. He was close to cashing in his dignity and taking Bryce to his new, rented bed to show Bryce he had hit the mark. He headed for the front door, instead, in the hope Bryce would take the hint and leave.

Bryce ignored him. "And while I'm out there searching for a guy named Biff, what will you be doing?" *The natural implication of the remark being that Charlie* wasn't *Biff.* Charlie held his tongue. He had already met his nastiness quota for the morning.

Bryce walked to the sliding glass door, which led to the tiny balcony—a glorified outdoor shelf—with the pitiful, dazed gait of a haggard man and looked at the view. Charlie knew what he saw. It was the dryer ventilator for the apartment across the way. The aperture stuck out of a large field of cream-colored stucco. Charlie had stared at it a zillion times. He had memorized all the places where the metal was dented, rusted, and scratched. "Will you see other men?" Bryce faced Charlie to get his answer. *A little redemption. Bryce implied Charlie could find someone else.* He halted the analysis there. He hated to think what Bryce's version of a someone else for Charlie looked like.

"I haven't thought that far. I don't envision it. Then again, am I going to be a flower on the wall and watch you dance? I don't know. Maybe. Maybe not." Charlie tried, for Bryce's sake, to look Bryce right in the eye and deliver the truth. "At some point, we'll both have to move on."

"Fifteen days ago, I left for work expecting to come home to the man I'd be with until one of us died. I knew we were facing something dreadful, but I was ready because I'd be facing it with you. *With* you. Nine hours later...."

"Seven years, fifteen days, nine hours, the four minutes it took to write a comment on a blog, the three it took to read it.... Hard to say which span of time wore on us the worst."

"Not the seven years. Those were the best years of our lives. How can you say those wore on us? Is that how you see them?" Charlie saw Bryce's last shred of hope erode. He had counted on using the duration of their union as a foundation to rebuild, and Charlie had just told him it was never there, that they had been living on top of a sinkhole that had swallowed them whole.

"Yes. I spent them with a man who'd rather have someone else. It's...devastating."

"You're terribly wrong. I don't know how to make you see it. I don't know how to regain your faith long enough to make you listen. I'm so sorry. I'm— Well, I'm ruined." He sounded like a man with pneumonia as he let out a tortured sigh. "And, as for your suggestion, right now, I don't see how I could drink coffee with another man, let alone...."

"Either way, spare me the details. And if you want to visit here, you should call first."

Bryce looked shattered. "I see. The wallflower doesn't want to be interrupted if he blooms and gives off pollen to a bee with a nice...stinger."

Charlie ignored Bryce's crude reference. He figured he owed Bryce a free cheap shot, after his own earlier snide remark.

There was a knock at the door.

Charlie knew it was the maintenance man, but Bryce stood at attention. He seemed to have trepidations about who was there to see Charlie.

Charlie opened the door to a surprise for the second time that morning. The maintenance man had seemed beyond middle-aged over the phone. It turned out, he was thirty-something with a commanding voice.

He was also extremely good-looking. He wore hiking boots with thick socks folded over them and a pair of dark cargo shorts that showed off fabulous knees and lower legs. His T-shirt was loose, but a twelve-pack was visible through the thin material that fell back against his skin. He was as tan as a person could be without being sunburned. Charlie's apartment must have been his first stop for the day. He smelled like he came directly from his shower.

"Charlie?"

Charlie extended his hand. "Grayson?"

"That's me." He strolled into Charlie's living room as though he had been there before, likely because he had, for other tenants. He carried a small duffel bag. Charlie assumed it was full of tools, but it looked like an overnight bag. And a hook-up.

Charlie had no interest in Grayson. The love of his life was standing fifteen feet away, near the balcony door, with wet eyelashes. Charlie's assessment of Grayson was mere observation.

"Right on time. Thanks for coming on such short notice," Charlie said.

"We aim to please," Grayson said.

Charlie glanced at Bryce and noticed he wasn't checking out Grayson, even for his own sake of observation. He was locked onto Charlie.

After what Bryce had said about Charlie online, Charlie couldn't see why Bryce was worried. And, anyway, Charlie didn't think Grayson was gay. Grayson had fully ignored Bryce, which, in tight quarters with no distractions in the room, never happened with gay men and Bryce. As eye-catching as Grayson was, any objective observer would say Bryce was better looking. Very few men had that extra something Bryce had that made him beyond handsome. He was rare and arresting and conspicuous. Grayson would be the first gay man Charlie could remember who looked right through Bryce as though he weren't there. Even the ones who played it cool stole glances to get the lay of the land. Some straight men checked out Bryce because they envied what he embodied. Grayson stared at Charlie's walls.

Still, one never knew, and Charlie caught Bryce watching him and Grayson closely. He figured Bryce assumed Charlie was interested in Grayson, and not the other way around since Charlie wasn't all of that.

Charlie was suddenly infuriated again with Bryce and Still Got Vinyl and Apaulogize. Collectively, they resided in Bryce, and Charlie wanted them all to leave. Before Grayson had knocked, Charlie sensed Bryce was headed out the door after he realized Charlie may not want to be interrupted carrying on with bees. Charlie had no plans to "receive bees" anytime soon. He just wished Bryce would leave.

"I haven't built the wall unit yet," Charlie said to Grayson. He grinned a little self-consciously. "It's still in the boxes." He felt Bryce staring him down. "When I do, I was thinking of anchoring it here." He pointed at a wall. "Am I good to drill here? Landlord said I had to ask first."

"Yeah, this is fine. It's the same wall everyone with this sized unit uses. Not sure why the landlord always makes people waste time with me first." Grayson knocked on the wall in places. "See? Internal wall with studs." He shrugged at the obvious. "Tell you what," he said. "Break out those boxes, and let's put her up."

"No. You sure?" Charlie said.

"Yep. I'm on the clock either way. And I live in the building. Not like I'm facing a long drive home after this." He chuckled.

He *had* come directly from his shower.

"All right, then. I'm not one to turn down help."

Grayson finally looked at Bryce. He might as well have looked at another wall. "I'm Grayson. Nice to meet you." He was extremely friendly and flashed a genuine smile, but he didn't cross the few steps to shake Bryce's hand. It was a perfunctory introduction, and that was all.

"Bryce. I was just leaving when you knocked."

"All right, take it easy." Another nice smile. He bent down to unzip his duffel bag. He had moved on from Bryce.

"Goodbye, Charlie," Bryce said.

"Bye." He thought of something else. "Bryce?"

Bryce was already out the door, but he didn't ignore Charlie. "Yeah?"

"Careful with Juliet. Don't push it with her."

"I won't. Push it, I mean."

"Just go in, fake it if you have to, but take your down time on the inside, where she can see you. You're this close. Don't let...anything ruin that."

The saddest smile Charlie had ever seen appeared on Bryce's face. "I got it. No worries."

Charlie figured his smile looked about like Bryce's. "Okay."

After Bryce left, Grayson said, "Boyfriend?"

"No." It was the first time Charlie admitted it aloud to anyone. He was too dazed to resent the blunt question.

"Good. Then he won't mind if we get to know each other."

Charlie was flabbergasted. He had no idea Grayson was gay. He hadn't missed the signals. There flat-out were none. He didn't know what to say. He was in no frame of mind to entertain advances.

"It's okay," Grayson said. "I'm in no rush. Let's get your wall unit squared away."

Five

Charlie was afraid to dial the number. He used a burner phone Bryce would be unable to trace, but, as with calling in sick to his job on days he was healthy and feeling that the lie, *because it was untrue*, sneaked through the phone to the other end and was detectable, he dreaded Bryce figuring out that it was Charlie who called. He had the awful feeling that dishonesty would lead to discovery.

It was Monday. Two days had passed since Bryce had left Charlie and Grayson to erect Charlie's wall unit. Charlie thought Bryce might fail to show up for work after his unexpected two-week pause. He hated to see Bryce screw up the other parts of his life because his relationship with Charlie had blown up in his face. Charlie told himself he merely wanted to know if Bryce was at his desk and that he shouldn't care anyway. He swore further to himself that, as soon as Bryce answered, Charlie would hang up and move on with *his* life.

But those were lies, or at least not all the truth. He wanted to hear Bryce's voice. He wanted to tell him not to look for Biff, not to move on from Charlie. But he knew that was pointless. He would settle for one-sided contact, in which he said nothing after Bryce picked up the phone, and for confirmation Bryce had dragged himself out of bed.

He dialed Bryce's work number.

It rang four times and went to voice mail. The greeting still announced Bryce would be out of the office until the previous Friday. Either he had returned to work and forgotten to update his message from the two weeks he had been out, or, far worse, he hadn't returned and, to boot, didn't think to remotely call in and edit the greeting, accordingly.

Dammit, Bryce.

He called the number again.

No answer.

Charlie debated walking out of his own job in Century City to drive to Santa Monica and drag Bryce to work, but it was his first day back, too. He was on firm footing with his boss, and he needed to keep it that way.

He hit the redial button on the cheap phone. He got lost in the ringing, which he expected to end where Bryce's voice mail message began. Mentally, he was already in his car, on his way to Santa Monica. In just a few more seconds, in his mind, anyway, he'd be stammering at Bryce's front door, with a lousy explanation for why he was there.

"This is Bryce." Charlie jumped a little in his seat. Bryce's live voice on the other end of the line sounded awake and ready to listen.

Charlie froze.

"Hello?" Bryce said.

Charlie felt foolish for assuming Bryce was so devastated by losing Charlie, he was too paralyzed to work. Bryce sounded like he had bounced into the office several hours earlier.

Charlie hung up. His face felt hot. *How could I have been so dumb?*

Charlie reverted to the reality he had ignored during that time after Grayson left him with his wall unit and before he dialed Bryce's number. For a fantastical two days, he had thought maybe it had all been a great misunderstanding and that Bryce found him worthy and disagreed with Still Got Vinyl and the rest. Bryce's upbeat tone told Charlie Bryce had taken Charlie's advice. He was at work, faking it maybe, but moving on. Biff likely wasn't too far in the distance in Bryce's future.

Charlie stared at the burner phone sitting on his desk. He had planned to dispose of it once his reconnaissance operation was complete. He had just confirmed that Bryce was at work. He could discard the phone.

Instead, he tucked the phone into the inside pocket of his blazer. He would keep it for a while.

———◦◦◦———

"This is Bryce." He answered the phone on the third ring.

Charlie hung up.

It was Wednesday, two days after Charlie had made his first call to Bryce from his burner phone. Charlie felt wicked. He had wanted Bryce to protect his career and was glad he was at his desk, but he had also hoped Bryce had relapsed and was writhing in pain in Santa Monica as Charlie was every second he was at home in Culver City. It appeared Bryce was moving along just fine.

Nevertheless, Charlie hung onto the phone. It seemed silly to throw it away after just three days.

———◆◇◆———

"This is Bryce."

Charlie waited. He wanted to hear Bryce say a few more words, even just, "This is Bryce," a second time.

It was Friday. Bryce had apparently packed in a full week at work after his two-week relationship-fallout break. Charlie was relieved and devastated.

Then he was shocked. "Charlie?" Bryce said on the other end of the phone.

Charlie's heart raced.

"Babe? Is that you?"

Charlie held his breath.

"If you called to make sure things are fine, they're not."

Charlie gripped the edge of his desk.

"I mean, don't worry. I'm here, doing my thing, every day, I promise, but I need you, Charlie."

I'm sure you do, but you need more, too. You need so much more than I can give you. You deserve more than what I am. I deserve more than what you gave me. Charlie choked up with tears.

"Babe? Come home? Please? We can get through it. I'll work at whatever it takes to make it right. I love you. More than ever."

Charlie hung up.

He couldn't take any more. He couldn't listen to any more of what would never be right. He told himself he had to move on.

He had no more cause to keep the burner phone. It was getting in the way.

He wasn't ready to get rid of it, though.

Why can't I let you go, Bryce? I'll keep the phone over the weekend, just in case, and then I'll destroy it.

Then something hit Charlie. He freaked out.

He couldn't remember if he had blocked the number on his phone before he had dialed Bryce. In fact, he was sure he had forgotten to do that. He had also stayed on the line long enough for Bryce to jot down the number.

——◦◇◦——

Charlie sprang to attention on his ragged couch.

His burner phone rang.

No one knew the number except Charlie.

And Bryce.

It was Sunday, two days after Charlie had blundered and let his phone number appear in Bryce's caller ID window.

Charlie's burner phone was shoddy, but it had caller ID, too. The window flashed the word RESTRICTED. No number appeared.

Is it you? How I want to hear your voice.

Charlie almost answered but realized that would be foolish. Unless Bryce heard him on the line, he couldn't *prove* the phone belonged to Charlie. Bryce had talked to Charlie on Friday, but Charlie had never said a word in return.

He let the phone ring. After the fourth chime, the phone went dark. If the caller stayed on the line, he, or an unlikely she, would get a mechanical, nondescript voice mail greeting.

After a few moments, Charlie checked, and he had no messages. He would never know for sure who it was, but he had to assume it was Bryce.

Charlie knew, then, that he had made his last call to Bryce on the burner phone. His caper was over.

He was about to take the device outside and drive over it several times with the front wheel of his motorcycle, but something stopped him.

Bryce might call again.

⸺◆⸺

Charlie stared at his own Facebook page in a quandary. It was Monday, the day after Bryce, or someone, had called Charlie's burner phone. It was also the four-week anniversary of Charlie reading Bryce's cruel advice to the cop. It was just over three weeks since Charlie had walked out on Bryce. After the previous week of calling Bryce every other day, Charlie accepted he needed to move on from Bryce for real. It meant he would have to finally confess to the world that he and Bryce were no more, for, in the time since Charlie had left, he had managed a miracle. He had avoided telling family or friends what had happened between him and Bryce. His Culver City existence was covert. He hadn't been ready to face the shame behind the reason for the split, nor could he tolerate recriminations and questions from his mother, who loved Bryce like another son. The hue and cry from her would be unbearable. She would call every day and harangue them both until she got answers. Charlie dreaded and almost feared the day she found out the truth. Until he had learned to live with it and own it, he kept out all intruders.

He had been able to get away with the secrecy because people texted and e-mailed and put life on blast and shared, but they sometimes went ages without really talking. The constant flow of texts and e-mails and selfies replaced the need for in-person contact. People had begun to rely on the time saved to do other things, to live a life less encumbered by interactions with others, to visit each other far less. And because Charlie only had a cell phone and his landline at work, when he was at home, he could be reached in an emergency whether he was on the couch with Bryce or on the floor in Culver City.

Strangest for Charlie was that his entire plot relied on one factor, without which his scheme would have been doomed, and that thing had weirdly come through for him: Bryce had hidden the truth too. For whatever reason, Bryce hadn't told anyone about their breakup. Charlie had braced for impact within a week of leaving, but he never got hit with anything from Bryce's brother or his parents. That's when he realized Bryce must also have been carrying on a charade and covering up that Charlie had moved out. Several peeks at Bryce's social media confirmed Charlie's suspicion. Pictures of Charlie were everywhere. Bryce's "in a relationship" status never changed. All of which meant he knew Charlie hadn't told anyone since there would be no point in keeping up appearances if Charlie had put it on blast that they weren't together anymore.

Charlie considered outing them both and announcing his bad news online. He hated to blindside Bryce again, but he didn't see a way around it.

He had barely logged onto any of his social media accounts since the dawn of the Culver City Era, checking in only long enough to give his sister's posts a few likes to keep everyone off his scent.

He stared at his profile picture, a close-up of him and Bryce someone else had snapped for them. Bryce in that photo mesmerized Charlie and drew him in, made him forget he was supposed to be working. Bryce had tilted his head in just the right way and leaned his right cheek onto Charlie's left cheek. The little bit of affection made Bryce close his eyes. The picture had been captured at just that moment. Bryce looked so in love.
With Charlie.

Charlie logged off Facebook and went back to work. He would deal with the truth another day.

He watched his burner phone.

After all the realizations he'd made, he still waited for it to ring. He carried the phone everywhere at work and moved it around with him from room to room at home, but it never rang.

On Tuesday, it never rang.

On Wednesday, it never rang.

On Thursday, it never rang.

On Friday, it never rang.

On Saturday, it never rang.

———◦◦◦———

Bits of plastic and silicon which had once been Charlie's burner phone crunched under Charlie's motorcycle wheel. It was Sunday, a week to the day after the burner phone had rung, and just a month after Charlie had moved to Culver City. The phone hadn't rung since it had that one and only time.

Charlie had made one more call *from* it, though, to Bryce's desk at work, early in the morning that same Sunday, the day he smashed the phone with his motorcycle, when he knew Bryce wouldn't be there to answer. He didn't know to what end he had called. He only knew that he couldn't *not* call.

That inability to restrain himself was the reason the phone was now in pieces on the pavement. That, and the bad news he had heard on Bryce's outgoing greeting. *Out of the office. Two weeks. Japan.* Probably with Matthias, about whom Bryce never made Charlie worry for even a second, but of whom Charlie was jealous.

Matthias, who "brainstormed brilliantly," Bryce had said.

Matthias, who once saved Bryce in a meeting when Juliet had caught him unawares. It had been so seamless, Juliet had thought they had planned it that way.

Matthias, who was single.

Matthias, who was straight but eye-catching, and who would make a pleasant traveling companion for two weeks in a strange, wonderful land, where Bryce, always in his element if navigating required another language, would enjoy having Matthias there to show off for. Under different circumstances, *Charlie* would have been Bryce's admirer on that trip.

Let's go dancing, Charlie would say.

We don't know anyone in Tokyo.

We know each other, Babe. Let's go.

A slow dance in their hotel room, to ease Bryce into it. Out all Friday night at a hot club. Sleeping naked on Saturday. Dinner and a stroll around the city. Making love until Monday meetings.

It was already Monday in Japan. Bryce and Matthias were in Tokyo as Charlie sat on his bike and destroyed his phone.

Charlie knew what the venture was about. Bryce had prepped the project for eight months. With Matthias. Which is how Charlie knew so much about Matthias's virtues. He had made cameo appearances at enough dinner-table conversations to give Charlie a through line. Charlie was happy for Bryce that he had remained in Juliet's good graces and had hit his stride and advanced to the next step, but he could think of no clearer signal that his plan for Bryce had worked. Bryce was diving into life without Charlie and making a good go of it.

"Does that feel better?"

It was Grayson.

Charlie had thought he was by himself on the side of their apartment building. He didn't answer. He stared at the mangled phone on the pavement.

"Driving over that thing isn't gonna make the person on the other end go away. From your head, I mean."

Charlie didn't look up.

"If he ever does leave, let me know." He walked away.

Grayson was right, Charlie thought. The only way to get Bryce out of his head was to move on the way Bryce did.

After nightfall, Charlie sat in bed with his laptop and opened his e-mail. He received an announcement about a one-night screening of *West Side Story* happening the following month. He had subscribed to that event announcer because it let him surprise Bryce with fabulous date nights. *Cool Hand Luke in two weeks, Babe. Easy Rider. The Godfather. Where do you find these? I'll never tell. Teasing. Lovemaking.*

On instinct, he turned to tell Bryce about *West Side Story* and remembered he was alone, that Bryce would never again be on the other side of the bed.

He bought one ticket for the movie.

He closed the laptop and tossed it aside.

He turned off the light and wrapped himself in his comforter. "Good night, Bryce," he said out loud. "Travel safely."

It wasn't the first time he had talked to Bryce, as though he was there.

Six

I t was Thursday night. The next day would be the two-month anniversary of Charlie's leaving Bryce, and chance still had it in for Charlie. It had led him to Bryce's Internet post on that fateful Monday before he had moved out, and it ran him headlong into Bryce on a date at the movies that Thursday night.

Charlie couldn't believe misfortune's stunning timing where he was concerned, but there was Bryce, in the concessions area, just a few people ahead of him in line for what Charlie knew would be a small popcorn, a box of ice cream bites, and a root beer, with someone auditioning to be Biff.

Or was he Biff? Had he already picked up the slack in the rent? Was he living in Charlie's house, enjoying time with Bryce on Charlie's couch, and sleeping in Charlie's bed? If Charlie had seen them sooner, he would have skipped his diet soda, and maybe his movie, but by the time he joined the queue and gathered his surroundings, it was too late. He couldn't suddenly leave the line. He thought it best to blend in and not do anything to draw their attention. He prayed they weren't all seeing the same movie.

He watched Bryce. He should have scoped out Biff while he had the chance to assess him, but he hadn't seen Bryce since the two-week mark in Culver City, hadn't heard his voice since the Japan voice mail four weeks earlier.

Charlie stared at Bryce as though he was the lone creature in the theater who could see, as though Bryce, if he caught him, wouldn't notice his desire.

It depressed Charlie to realize he had once been the sole being to have all the rights in the world when it came to Bryce, a man who attracted attention anywhere he went, and who ignored it all for Charlie. *He had been Charlie's.*

The line moved up a little and interrupted Charlie's reverie. Charlie inched up without calling attention to himself.

He checked out Biff. Biff was tall and pale with a contrasting dark haircut that suited his angular face. He was almost as handsome as Bryce. He was handsomer than Charlie. He was just about all of that.

He apparently found himself funny. He said something and laughed. Bryce managed a courtesy grin at Biff's joke, but Charlie saw no joy. He looked nothing like he had the Sunday they had earned their motorcycle licenses and celebrated, with hope in the air about what they were on the verge of, excited and eager not to jinx it but trying it on and enjoying the way it fit. At least, Charlie had thought so. He had been forced to learn there were things about him that would never fit Bryce.

Bryce turned his way. Charlie made no pretense that he hadn't already been staring. He looked right at Bryce.

Bryce froze. He appeared guilty and caught.

They held each other captive with unbroken gazes. Charlie sensed that Biff talked at Bryce's temple, but Bryce didn't seem to hear him.

Bryce recovered first. He waded through the people who stood between Charlie and him. Biff was forced to do an awkward zigzag on Bryce's tail.

"Hi, Charlie. How are you?" Bryce stood close. "What are you doing here? Are you alone?"

Biff chuckled. "That's three quick questions. You two know each other?"

"Yeah, I'm Charlie." He offered his hand. Biff's hand was a vise. Somehow, its firm, confident grip hurt Charlie emotionally, though.

"Trevor. Nice to meet you."

Trevor. Not Biff. Not a theory but a man, on a date with Charlie's soul mate, in practice.

"What movie are you seeing?" Bryce said. He was the only one not bothering with a fake smile.

"*West Side Story.*" *Please don't be seeing that.*

"That's playing? How'd I miss that?"

Thank God.

"One-night-er. You had to buy the tickets online." Charlie felt himself fade back again, as he had the night he bought his ticket, to his and Bryce's house. They shouted out plans from one room to the other, chose their seats on the very same computer that had destroyed their relationship, tossed around dinner ideas, and sang show tunes.

"I never liked musicals too much," Trevor said.

Charlie and Bryce ignored him. They both seemed to be someplace Trevor wasn't.

The line moved.

"You never said. Are you here alone?" Bryce said.

"I can help who's next!" a cashier called.

"That's us," Trevor said.

Us.

The next cashier took Charlie at the same time. He was two stations away from Bryce and Trevor. Charlie used a prolonged perusal of the elevated menus stretched high along the wall behind the cashier to observe Bryce and Trevor through his peripheral vision. It was unmistakable. Bryce watched him. Charlie resolved not to lower his eyes and look their way.

Jealousy took over. Charlie used a little revenge to ease it. He ordered two drinks and a large popcorn, something Bryce knew he would never put into his body, to give the impression he was on a date too.

He paid for his snacks and turned in the opposite direction of Bryce and Trevor to leave the concessions area. Every other step, he resisted the urge to turn around and look at them. He was glad for his nice ass in case they looked at him.

———◆◆———

Charlie spotted Bryce, alone on a bench in the lobby of the movie theater, and practically threw his head back and rolled his eyes. He didn't feel like dealing with any more of Bryce and Trevor on a date. Bryce saw Charlie, too, though, so Charlie checked himself. Bryce stood to meet Charlie.

Charlie surprised himself and spoke first. "Where's Trevor?" he asked. He hadn't meant to be so obvious. A pall from the heartbreaking way *West Side Story* ended hung over him. His emotions were ripe and electric. He was unable to be tempered and less straightforward.

"He left before the movie started. Hopped the Red Line home. He could tell we, or at least I, had unfinished business."

"Oh. I'm not sure what to say."

"I was relieved. I…I don't know. You never did say. Are you alone?"

"Is that why you're sitting here? To see if I was alone?"

"To see you, period. If someone else is here, in the men's room, or whatever, I'll try not to make it awkward. I just wanted to see you."

"While you were on a date?" He was unfair, but he didn't care. He was jealous and carrying around the sad strains of *West Side Story's* flute-infused, closing-credits version of "Somewhere". He had spent the whole movie missing Bryce through Shakespearean balcony-scene metaphors, star-crossed love, sexy dances, funny lines, and perfect music that invoked opera and theater, two things they both loved. He imagined Bryce and Trevor in their movie, occasionally glancing at each other at meaningful moments in the film and affectionately resting their hands on each other's thighs. *Please don't be falling in love in there*, he had repeated in his mind through *West Side Story*.

"A date that ended the minute you appeared."

Charlie barely felt better. Bryce had just confirmed it was a date he and Trevor had been on. After a moment of awkward silence, he said, "It's none of your business. I need to go get my bike."

He started for the lobby exit. He gave the impression he might be swinging back around to the theater to pick up a date taking care of men's room business, who would hop on the back of his motorcycle and head home with him to Culver City, as long a ride as to where Charlie and Bryce had lived in Santa Monica.

That shared motorcycle ride would gall Bryce and was a bonus to the rest of what Charlie tried to extract from the moment. Charlie and Bryce both rode motorcycles, but Bryce loved jumping onto Charlie's bike with him. Charlie pushed speed limits and had a far better handle on his machine. Bryce got a thrill from riding at high speed with his arms around Charlie.

Bryce followed him out the lobby door.

Outside, they went the same way. Charlie realized they had both parked in a neighborhood full of unadvertised street parking they had used often as a couple when they went to that theater. There would be no shaking Bryce.

Charlie could have used their moment together to advance his fake-date scheme with painful words. Instead, he opted for, "Where did you meet Trevor?" Jealousy had usurped his objective.

"At Amoeba, in the R and B section. Near Earth, Wind and Fire."

Charlie's favorite.

"He asked for my number. I gave it to him out of frustration, with us and with all things Culver City."

With Japan and Matthias and a good-looking Trevor showing great taste in music, admiring Bryce while he did it, Charlie was a bit surprised Bryce even remembered he lived in Culver City.

"When he called, I came clean, but he suggested a movie, for fun. It was the only date I've been on, I swear."

"You don't have to swear anything to me."

"I know, but I want to. That's why I've been waiting in the lobby almost since you went into *West Side Story*. To tell you I didn't finish my date."

The gesture was lost on Charlie. Charlie had just one thing on his mind. He summoned the courage and admitted what he hated. "Trevor's handsome."

"Is he? I don't know. Whatever." Bryce stopped. He gently reached for Charlie's arm.

Charlie stopped too. *What did Bryce want? He had moved on. Why couldn't he leave Charlie alone?*

They were on a side street with no lights. The dark gave them privacy. "Charlie, I have so much I want to say, but I don't think you'll want to hear it."

"How do you know?" Charlie was disingenuous in implying he'd listen. There wasn't much about Bryce's new life Charlie wanted to hear.

"Because. You sent me away to find out things, and then you keep me away. I wonder if you'll ever let me share what I've discovered."

Charlie didn't know what to think.

"If we hadn't run into each other, I'm sure you would have been happy to go your whole life never seeing me again."

It wasn't true, but Charlie was at a loss as to how to tell Bryce. He didn't know where he fit in with Bryce anymore, how to be the right kind of ex-partner.

"For all I know, somebody's waiting for you back there. I guess your bike has two helmets locked on it tonight."

No, just one.

Charlie walked again. He needed to get farther into the dark. He wanted to flee the abyss of inadequacy he felt himself falling into, but Bryce was right by his side.

At the next narrow intersection, Charlie veered away, toward his motorcycle. Bryce grabbed his hand. "Where are you going?"

"My bike's that way." He let Bryce keep his hand. It reminded him of when Bernardo, in *West Side Story*, cornered Anita in the shadows of a stairwell. *Would he and Bryce kiss the way Bernardo and Anita had?* He suddenly wanted it.

"Don't go," Bryce said.

They kissed and quickly gained speed. They necked in the dark longer than they had kissed at Charlie's apartment six weeks earlier. It went on for several minutes, as they fell into comfortable, familiar rhythms.

A horn honked in the distance.

As in Culver City, it was Charlie who pulled away. "Bryce, we can't date each other on the rebound *from* each other."

"Dammit," Bryce said. He stepped back. "See what I mean? We're never going to get anywhere. We're going to be stuck in that cul-de-sac forever. Unless you've already found a way out with someone else." He started to leave but stopped himself. "Sometimes, I think I'm going to pay for what I did for the rest of my life, *with* the rest of my life. If you ever loved me, you'll understand how I think of my life as having to do with yours and what your being gone means to my existence and what I always thought my being gone would mean for your existence. Good night, Charlie." He walked into the shadows.

Charlie saw well enough to know he didn't look back.

———◆———

It was still Thursday. An image of Bryce came to Charlie over and over in his kitchen in Culver City. It was of Bryce walking into the dark earlier that night, away from Charlie.

Charlie had made the long ride home on his bike, thinking the whole way about Bryce, about seeing him with Trevor and walking with him in the blackness and kissing him.

He also thought about defiance, something he saw in Bryce, even in the dimness of the side streets. Right there in the middle of the road, *as he crossed it*, Bryce had seemed to go straight from bargaining to acceptance in working through grief and to have skipped depression altogether.

Charlie had seen plenty of denial and even anger in the early days. Bryce had tried to bargain in Culver City and on the burner phone. Throughout, there had been sadness, but Bryce didn't appear to be suffering from the depression that had plagued Charlie. Bryce had shifted into acceptance the moment Charlie had declared that they couldn't use each other to get over each other. Charlie realized he should move to acceptance too.

A refrain fought its way to the front of his mind. What was it? Something Bryce had said.

We're never going to get anywhere.

Once it made itself known, it circled around and around inside Charlie's head. He stared at the microwave for ten minutes without moving. Suddenly, he snapped out of it and grabbed his car keys.

Seven

The phone rang eight times. Bryce never picked up. Charlie called again.

"Hello?" Bryce answered on the eighth and final ring. He had always had his cell phone set for the full eight rings, he had said, because he didn't want to miss calls from Charlie. Charlie assumed that had changed and that Bryce hadn't gotten around to updating his settings. *Or maybe he didn't want to miss someone else's calls.* Charlie figured also that his face no longer appeared during those eight rings and that Bryce had stripped Charlie from his phone. Either way, Charlie knew Bryce recognized the number and had let it ring. The tone of his voice betrayed that he had answered reluctantly.

Charlie suddenly regretted the call. "I'm sorry," he said. "I shouldn't have called so late. I'll talk to you some other time."

"Why did you call?"

"Never mind. I'll let you go."

"Tell me why you called."

Charlie sucked it up. He figured he had less than nothing to lose. "After the way things ended at the movies, I was wondering."

"What?"

"If…this was a bad time. For me to come over. Like I said, though, it's late—"

"I'd like to see you."

He sounded like a school principal who hoped to scold Charlie. Charlie wished he hadn't called. "Are you sure? What about Trevor?" He couldn't believe he was hiding behind Trevor as a last-ditch way out of the call. Then again, he did want to know the answer to the question. *What about Trevor?*

"What about him?"

"Maybe you reconnected. You know, I'll just let you go."

"I didn't reconnect with Trevor, and I thought you were coming over."

Charlie didn't respond.

"What time will you be here?" He sounded like the principal again.

Charlie rang the doorbell. "I'm here now."

Bryce opened the door. "I didn't hear your bike."

"I'm not on my bike. I rode it home and came back in my car. I'm parked in front of Janey's house. I wasn't sure I was gonna knock."

"Oh."

They contemplated each other.

"Come in," Bryce finally said.

Charlie followed Bryce into their old living room, the principal's office, and was gut-punched by the degree to which things had changed: not an iota. It was all still there. Enlarged vacation photos in artsy frames on the walls, coasters depicting classic films, fine knickknacks, and their couch, which was vast and deep enough for two grown men to spoon comfortably and doze, or make love, as they watched football games on TV all day Sunday.

Seeing the couch was especially tough on Charlie. They had bought it together the week they moved into that house, and it had been Location Zero for so much they had perpetrated as a couple. It was a confessional, a place of forgiveness and friendship. It had lured them into days of hooky from work when a marathon of their favorite show was on cable. It had provided the playground for light sex, which led to heavier play in the bedroom.

Charlie regretted the impulsivity which had brought him there. For the first time since he left Bryce, he wished he were at his place in Culver City, where everything was rented and strange, but where he was safe. Worse, standing in what had been their home, he was becoming upset, at himself, mostly. Just a few hours earlier, Bryce had been on a date with another man, someone he may have brought back to that very living room. Bryce could have put moves on Trevor on *their* couch and transitioned to *their* bedroom. That was all possible because Charlie had set Bryce free.

What was he doing there? He vaguely remembered it had something to do with Bryce saying they were never going to get anywhere. He had seen a thin thread of hope in that statement, as though Bryce thought they were still on the path somewhere, but once he stood before Bryce and tried to shape it into something he could make sense of and say aloud, he felt silly, as though he had raised his hand in class to make a brilliant point, not realizing he had misinterpreted the text that was the focus of the lesson, and ended up making a fool of himself in front of fifty people.

He asked the most provocative question he could think of, hoping Bryce would throw him out. "If Trevor hadn't bailed, would he be here now? On that couch?" He pushed it. "Or in the bedroom?"

"No, even though that's as much none of your business as my questions to you were none of mine."

"You're right." *Do something about it. Send me on my way.*

Bryce moved closer. "I don't mind. Everything I have, even my business, is yours, Charlie, even if you don't want it. So, let me tell you again, since you seem determined to forget it. Even though we're destroyed, I am nowhere near ready to move on like that. I wish you would stop suggesting it."

The rebuke stung. Charlie gave up his fool's errand. "I should leave."

"I know *you've* moved on. I can feel it."

Bryce stopped Charlie cold with that statement.

Charlie tried to keep up the game he started at the movies. He wanted to withhold and elude Bryce and make him wonder and regret moving so quickly to acceptance, but he was out of steam. He couldn't muster what it took beyond the false signals he had managed at the theater. Those had fallen into his lap, and he had gone along and accepted fortune's help. He had no idea how to mislead Bryce in a premeditated way. They had never been that way with one another. They were best friends, who tended to be polite, old-fashioned, tender, and forthcoming in their relationship. At least, Charlie had always been open.

Charlie was stymied.

When no response came, Bryce showed shades of the junkie he had been in Culver City, except he stood his ground and didn't pace. He was more like a junkie who had gotten clean and accepted his new life.

Acceptance.

"I have no pride, Charlie. I have no shame in telling you I've driven myself crazy every night imagining you were so angry about that vile post, you were in bed with someone else, with someone you knew deserved you more than I did."

Charlie wanted to stop the world there. *That was a very different kind of acceptance.* Charlie had been miserable for eight weeks, existing more than living, and aimlessly searching for ways to prove to himself he had a life. Bryce's profession of jealousy made him feel alive again. Whether he liked it or not, the vibrancy in his life came from his love for Bryce. Anything that reinforced that made him feel better, regardless of their status as a couple.

He was rug-burned, though, and cautious. He couldn't give in at the sound of a few pleasing, taunting words.

"I'm not talking about revenge sex," Bryce said. "I'm talking about intimacy, love, a connection, your searching for better than what I gave you and finding it, and it's made me obscenely resentful and envious and desirous."

Charlie's heart soared.

"I assume he fell in love with you right away, the way I did."

Charlie was dizzy thinking about the night he and Bryce fell in love, on their first date, and how it led right away to the first time they made love. Each had known he loved the other at the *exact same instant.* It was an enormous and complete love that had formed with stunning synchronicity. It happened the moment in *Vertigo* when Kim Novak emerged in the image of Jimmy Stewart's dead love and bowled him over with the immensity of it. Charlie and Bryce had turned to each other and understood they loved each other.

Later that night, their first time together was more a culmination of that instant in the theater than it was a moment for its own short-term purpose of physical satisfaction. They had blended as lovers who had known only each other, for thousands of days and not merely for one night. It had been magic.

"Every night in our bed, I see him in my mind, and every night, he discovers you anew and falls in love with you again," Bryce said. He took half a step forward.

"I try to look away from the torturing images of you. I remember well what you look like when you're in love and giving yourself, and I can't bear it. If a lifetime goes by, I'll never forget how you love, Charlie."

Charlie was uneasy hearing talk of the physical, visual side of his way of loving.

"I'll have to find a way, while always remembering you, to cope with the truth that you're not giving yourself to me, anymore. You'll be giving all of what you have and what you are, in a purer form, untainted by mistrust, to him. There's nothing left for me."

Charlie almost gave in and confessed, about the phone calls and about how he had had the identical fears and lain in his bed nights in Culver City, a dried-up wallflower, a withered, dead bud, tortured, too, because he assumed Bryce and a bevy of beautiful men were having wondrous sex all the time, sex that was worthy of their magnificence and grace, but he had no desire to relitigate the question of his looks. He was worn out, by the damage and by the worry he felt setting in. What if Bryce had no good answers? What if what Charlie wanted wasn't there? What if it was impossible to revive dead petals? The flight pattern of his soaring heart dropped a thousand feet. He hoped his heart wasn't headed into a nosedive.

"Who is he, Charlie?" Bryce said. "Did you meet around the time you stopped calling me from that other phone?"

Charlie exhaled. "Those calls."

"Were you trying to tell me about him, each time you called? Did you lose your nerve? Is that why you hung up without saying a word?"

Charlie shook his head. He couldn't talk about those calls.

"I recognized your breathing that third time, when you let me talk to you. I knew, then, that I had been right, that it had been you the other two times. I couldn't wait for you to call again, but you never did. I must have scared you off when I tried to call you that Sunday."

It was Bryce. In that moment, Charlie felt something shift. In his favor. Charlie wasn't ready to confess the rest, to admit to the call he made when he learned Bryce was in Japan. "Why did you restrict the number when you called me?" Charlie said.

"On the outside chance it wasn't you. And...."

"What?"

"I presumed you were entrenched in your new situation and didn't want to hear from me. Someone had fallen for you. That, naturally, won your attention."

"Oh."

"Did you love him immediately? Because he was perfect? And kinder than I was, as he would have to be? Is that why you wouldn't tell me about him? You didn't want to be cruel? I don't mean to start anything, Charlie, but you've already been cruel, from the moment you left and every day after that. You might as well finish me off. I have no hope of surviving the comparison between him and me after what I did. I just want to know that you're happy. I've sensed the nails in my coffin. Maybe I need you to make me feel their pinch to move on."

"Bryce—"

"I've felt so inadequate and so thoroughly left out of whatever secret and perfect world you and he created. I've pictured you two laughing all the time, at me and at life, which itself became something you were united against because it had tried to trick you into unhappiness, but you beat it. You two against the world. I've only ruled out Grayson. That leaves a large universe of possible foes."

Of course, you ruled out Grayson, who is far too good for me. Charlie's heart was about to crash-land. It was barely aboveground. "What makes you so sure about Grayson?"

"He was nice to you, like people always are, but he didn't flirt, which means he's either straight or gay and looking for something convenient, which isn't anything you'd put up with."

No, I wouldn't put up with it, but I'm in love with you, so none of that matters.

"If there's one thing I know, it's that you attract flirts. Everywhere we go. On the dance floor, at the farmer's market, in the motorcycle shop. If a man's gay and searching for something real, he'll flirt with you and try to impress you. It worried me the whole time we were together. But I was proud all the time, too, of how charming and cute and goddamned appealing you were and are."

"I beg to differ."

"Of course, you do. That's the point, although you're a tad out of character right now. You're not very nice, making whoever your new man is wait while you visit an ex-lover, late at night."

Charlie raised his eyebrows in shock.

"But I don't care because I hate him, for having you and for...."

"For what?" Charlie could barely speak.

"For what he symbolizes. My causing it all. He's there because I'm not, and you're happier for it." Bryce moved ever nearer to Charlie. "I had always thought we were not only perfect for each other but best for one another. It turns out, all the time we were together, there was somebody else out there who was better for you. Other than losing you, that's the worst part. Even when it's no longer fresh and unsustainably exciting between you, as it must be now, it will never be as tarnished as I made us. I guess I should be glad for that and pleased that you're happy."

Charlie knew then that he would never get over Bryce or his whole way of being.

"I expected to meet him tonight and for him to brag to my face that my misfortune was his great luck and to mock my foolishness and my mistake and to try to kick my ass and tell me to stay away from you and to boast about the accident of his existence in your life, except it turns out it's no accident. You're meant to be."

"You expected that tonight?" *And you hung around anyway, ready to fight.*

"Yes. Is that why you're here? Because you two agreed that tonight was the night you would tell me you've moved on with him? What's next? Our family and friends and Facebook pages?"

Charlie was flummoxed.

"Okay, then, you're moving on." He inched closer to Charlie. "Will you tell him we kissed at the movies while he was waiting inside for you to come back with your bike?"

"I—"

"It was torture being allowed to kiss you tonight, Charlie, knowing it would never happen again and that I was the interloper in another man's world with you. Do you know how strange that is? To be an intruder in your life? For seven years, I was the one who always felt lucky you were coming home with me. Challengers buzzed about, intrigued by the great conversationalist, who makes people feel like they're the only one in the room when they're talking and he's listening, who sings along to whatever's playing with the voice of an angel, who's aware of none of it. I was always secretly smug toward those who passed you up before we met. Their stupidity was my gain. Now, I'm one of them."

Charlie didn't feel like a man who had supposedly mastered the art of words. "I don't know."

"Why did you let me kiss you?"

Charlie wasn't sure. There were a million reasons.

"I almost didn't answer the phone tonight, but I can't stay away from you, Charlie. I'll take what I can get."

Charlie couldn't breathe. He was about to relent, but Bryce pushed for an answer to his earlier question.

"Why did you come here?"

Charlie pondered his shoes for a long moment. He glanced at the poster-sized photo of the two of them in Helsinki that hung on the wall behind Bryce. Finally, he looked at Bryce. All he had to offer was the truth.

"To admit I was unfair and didn't let you explain what happened. I gave you one shot at talking—that damned post. It was hard for me to see it at the time—you hurt me bad—but I think maybe I was unfair, walking out without a conversation. We fought, but we didn't talk. You didn't get a vote. I figured what you said online *was* your vote and that there was nothing more to say. I couldn't see what there was to add. I was devastated."

He glanced at the Helsinki photo again, a welcoming hiding place. He took refuge in the Lutheran Cathedral on Senate Square.

He often wondered what kind of challenge the many steps that led from the square to the church would present Rocky Balboa. It had been a Tuesday in early November. The clock on the dome read: 8:18. The sun rose late that time of year, so far north. Charlie and Bryce had gone to the square during the earliest light. They had the plaza to themselves. It had taken them a while to find someone to snap their picture. Most Helsinkians had rushed past on their way somewhere out of the cold. Tourists in November were rare.

Bryce watched him stare at the portrait and said nothing. Charlie could no longer avoid the worst of what he had gone there to say. "In retrospect, I'm embarrassed by how harsh I was. And reactive. I guess I came here to admit I hurt you when I wouldn't listen and maybe made a grave error. Some of this is my fault." He was filled with nervous guilt. "You had your conversation on the Internet, and I've been having mine with myself and some carpet in Culver City. Neither way is good."

"It's strange and wonderful to hear you talk like you used to and like you love me," Bryce said. "It makes me feel like I matter, like we're not in enemy camps. I've missed being on the same side with you. Terribly. It's noble of you to try to tie up loose ends fairly before you embark on your new relationship."

Charlie suddenly felt such pain and empathy for Bryce. He was ashamed that he had, in his own way, humiliated Bryce. He had fled and shone a bright light on Bryce's mistakes, which were the beginning of what tore them apart. Charlie finally understood his own actions were the end. Instead of working through Bryce's blunder with him, Charlie had called it betrayal and forced Bryce to forfeit his rights. It was Bryce who had been detained in the principal's office the entire time, waiting for Charlie to come along and say, "It's okay. You can go home now," only he had hoped to hear, "*Let's* go home, together, and stay in it to the end. I'll teach you. You teach me." But Charlie had deserted Bryce. Bryce had been half right in Culver City. Charlie hadn't lied about trusting Bryce all those years, but his actions had turned him into a liar. He had behaved like a man who had lost faith.

"What did you want to tell me at the movies?" Charlie said.

"I'm scared to say it now. In my head, I barely get through the very beginning of it, and you storm out."

"Because of how I left before." Charlie glanced one more time at Helsinki. "I was embarrassed. I felt like you had been tolerating me for years. I had to end it immediately."

"I know."

"Tell me. I'll try to listen."

"You're not promising, though."

"I can't. I don't know what you're going to say, and I won't know what I can take until I hear it."

"And if you can't? Will you go home to whoever's waiting and tell him all about it? I'd prefer not to be the subject of any further ridicule you two may share about me. I'm not sure it matters anymore, anyway. You've moved on."

"It matters, and I said I would try to listen."

"All right. In a way, I have nothing more to lose."

It was the same thing Charlie had thought when he appeared at Bryce's door.

Bryce held his breath for a moment. Finally, he said, "You were right to leave me when you did. It was long overdue."

Charlie's face fell. His heart crashed and bled out.

Bryce touched his arm. "I know you want to beat it out of here, but don't. Please don't. Let me explain. Give me a fighting chance, Charlie. Whoever he is, he's already won. He shouldn't be afraid to wait long enough for me to say these words."

Charlie stared at him.

"What I have to say is going to be much harder on me, Charlie. Trust me."

Charlie didn't respond, but he didn't leave. Something told him he should stay, that he should let himself hear what Bryce was about to say, that even if it was the worst thing that had happened in two months, it *should* happen. He didn't understand his own thinking, but he stood still and waited.

"As horrible as it has been," Bryce said, "I have to admit that when you left, you forced me to see something dreadful. I've been wrong for seven years. I have to live with that now. Maybe I'm selfish for making you listen to me wallow in it, but I don't expect you to absolve me of anything. I don't deserve it. I just need to tell you that you were right. I owe you that much."

Charlie didn't know what to feel. What was Bryce saying? Charlie longed for his floor in Culver City.

"After I saw you at your new place, and you wouldn't come home, I read my post again and again and again. From that awful printout. I deleted the one online. The replies went with it."

Charlie was glad to hear that, but he wished Bryce would make his point and without talking about that horrid post.

"I read that ugliness for days."

Charlie could barely take it.

"Page after page. I saw what you saw. It was ghastly and mortifying, maybe even more to me than to you. I drowned in the words until I was inured to their wretchedness, to the extent it was possible. After a while, I saw them with a more detached eye, you know?"

Charlie nodded.

"I realized something. When we met, I had an immature outlook and never bothered to grow up."

"I don't get it." He was about to burst with dread.

"When we talked that first time, at least from my end, it was because I was drawn to you. *Because.* But, being stupid, I had kind of assumed that since you weren't like others I had dated, it meant that I liked you and then loved you, *despite* who we were, and that you didn't quite have 'all that' because you were different from my typical narrow type. I let that permanently define you. I didn't have a clue about how I truly felt, about what drove my attraction to you."

He moved as close as possible to Charlie as an ex-lover could without encroaching. "When I saw you that first day, *saw you*, I didn't want to let you get away. I was naturally turned on by you and tagged along everywhere you went, when you came up for air from your music and your phone. Even when you were talking to other people in the class, I gate-crashed. Don't you remember that I always looked for you?"

"Yeah. I do." And he did. He thought it strange he had forgotten that the day he read Bryce's post. He had only remembered that they sometimes talked. He hadn't recalled that

Bryce usually created those opportunities, on the hunt for Charlie. Humiliation had blocked it out. He realized right then, though, that the dynamic wherein Bryce chased Charlie had given Charlie the confidence to try for a relationship with someone as striking as Bryce. It had made him feel deserving, then and always. Its effect had been lasting but somehow forgotten in a dark moment.

Charlie hated himself for the oversight. He had been blinded by shame, by words on a screen, which were black and white and stark and powerful, and by what Still Got Vinyl and Apaulogize—and Bryce—thought of him. He had catapulted himself into a reality that rang truer to those cold words, which was that he was not good enough for Bryce.

They had been caught in the most glorious perfect storm of the Internet. Bryce typed, and Charlie read, and neither had talked about what was "said". Bryce's words had planted the seeds of misunderstanding, but lack of faith had grown the confusion. It was hard to have faith in the latent good intentions in online chatter, which seemed to speak plainly. Charlie had fallen prey to custom. An Internet post was finite, was designed to be taken at face value, and was often succinct, to lead to that end. Even if the writer hoped to infuse nuance, the average comments were viewed as literal spouting off. They meant no more than what the letters spelled.

Charlie could read between the lines, but what he saw depended on the words *in* the lines. The figurative space between the lines Bryce had written was narrow. There wasn't much room for interpretation. Charlie wasn't sure all the faith in the world could overwrite what he had seen in black and white on his computer screen. Bryce had been indelicate with his words and never had a chance. Neither of them did.

Charlie was sure that if he and Bryce were to survive, he had to begin to forget the words on the screen. He had to listen to what Bryce said. He had to remember that, offline, faith in Bryce had always been easy.

"Right away," Bryce said, "I became attached to you in a way that was unbreakable, that is still unbroken."

Charlie wanted to believe it.

"Fate or luck or coincidence threw us into the same class, and we responded because we are drawn to one another. It was always a 'because of' relationship. There was never any 'despite' between us. I wish I had realized it before it was too late."

Charlie closed his eyes. "Bryce."

Bryce put his arms around Charlie's waist. "I know I'm violating someone else's rights, but I don't care. I need to make sure you know, no matter what happens, that I believe *you and I* were meant to be. This has been the only relationship I've ever wanted or tried to be worthy of because you, Charlie, *are* exactly '*all* of that'. All of it. No one else *could* be because they're not you. *You* are the mold, not the others. I saw it that first day. I saw in you everything I ever wanted, everything I had never seen before that day. There was a self-assurance in you, in your eyes and your walk and your gentle smile, and I had to have you and that quiet swagger of yours."

"Swagger? Me?" Charlie smiled for the first time since he had walked through the door.

"Yes, you." Bryce smiled too. "It was damned sexy. I thought, who *is* he?"

"I don't know about that." He felt self-conscious. His grin showed it.

"I do. It's why you left. It's how you could stay gone, even if you hated it. You said it yourself, that day. 'I don't want to leave. I have to.' It's subconscious, more than anything. I don't even think you work at it. It comes from the way you are."

"The way I am?"

"You're down-to-earth. People want to be near you. Everybody's always showing you where the mayonnaise is in the store and helping you pay for parking if you have a little trouble with one of those stupid machines and building wall units with you."

"Or maybe they want to show me how to use the gear shift on a motorcycle when I didn't ask them?" Charlie smiled.

"Guilty."

They did an absent-minded slow dance.

"It's uncanny. Like, one minute it's you, and the next, someone appears, as though they were watching the whole time, waiting, oblivious to me farther up the aisle or across the lobby, also watching and waiting. You must feel strangely powerful knowing people seek you out without you sending up flares. But you don't seem to see it. It makes you rare. And alluring, a wonderful find. You're damned handsome, Charlie. The best treasure there ever was."

Charlie was mesmerized. He had never thought about it. He just lived.

"You always say people stare at me. I guess they do. I can't see what good it does. Chiseled cheekbones are meaningless. They don't say anything. They're never the catalyst to meaningful discourse. They don't enrich the soul. Your charm and your warmth say everything. And the first time I spoke to you, you *listened*, to *me*. You looked me in the eye in a very different way. It's the way you look at everybody. Like you're trying to get inside, like you'll crawl in if you have to, to pull out what a person needs help to release. Only, I was lucky because, on top of that, you loved me."

Charlie suddenly felt silly about the day he left and how he had missed entirely what Bryce had tried to tell him about supermodel looks and about how someone being different made them better and right and not defective and about how the physical and the emotional *did* converge for Bryce and turn Charlie into someone special and about how Bryce sometimes wished he were Charlie, but he was also overwhelmed by the significance of what Bryce said, of how much he was loved for who he was, and of how much he loved Bryce's soul.

"I'm paying the price of a lifetime," Bryce said, "for getting it way too late that I had been waiting my whole existence, not just for someone like you, but for *you*. You're the most beautiful person I know, and I thought you were a paradox in my life because you were different from others, when, really, you were a confirmation of what was supposed to be. There were no mishaps. Everything clicked because it was as it should have been. Those challenges I thought we met weren't difficult because they weren't *real*. I assumed we leapt over obstacles instead of understanding that we came together because there were no hurdles. And now you're moving on, past me, to someone who understood you from the start, to travel on a road that's flat and endless. I'm sure he'll never make the mistakes I've made."

Charlie relented. "Your imagination has run wild, just as, shamefully, mine did the week I left." Charlie felt the shackles loosen with that admission. "I told you I expected to be alone a long while and that you couldn't be replaced. The flower never gave off pollen. Not to anyone. Anyone. If anything, I've become a shriveled-up bloom with dead petals and no color, looking for water and for life again."

Bryce's eyes moistened. "I can't take false hope, Charlie. I need the truth. I've missed you in spans measured by seconds. Please don't toy with me."

"That *is* the truth. I haven't moved on. I don't think I ever will. For what that's worth. I love you. The only man I've held hands with or kissed or made love with or thought about or dreamt about or cried about in the last seven years is standing right here."

"Charlie. Charlie. Please. Is this real?"

"Yes. It's real, Bryce. It's real. I love you. I could never move on from you. And I never said I did. You said it. I only let you think for a short while because it kept me safe. I can't explain it any other way."

Bryce blinked several times and stared out at nowhere, unbelieving. It was as though he were a man—sure he had been diagnosed with a fatal disease—hearing someone walk in and tell him he had been given the wrong test results and was going to live.

"I can't believe you were *that* convinced I had fallen in love with another man."

"I *was* that convinced. I figured it had to be. I saw you running from me, from us, to what you deserved, which was something better. It was the only path that made sense."

"No. Being with anyone but you makes *no* sense."

Bryce leaned all the way in and kissed Charlie. He started gently, testing the possibilities. When Charlie gave no sign of shutting him down, he bore in and feasted.

They ate and licked and bit and sucked and caressed each other's mouths until Charlie's head was spinning with dazzlement. He pulled away to catch his breath and not because he objected to their kissing.

"Oh, Babe, all I want to do is give you water," Bryce said. "Let me give you life again. Please come back and give me life. I'm withering away without you."

Their lips brushed as they talked. They continued their dance, turning a slow circle. Charlie felt lighter than he had in a long while. He let Bryce's words form the song for their dance. It wasn't *West Side Story*. It was better because it was real.

Bryce drew Charlie closer. "Babe, I'm so sorry. In the moment I posted that ugliness, I was excited for us and excited to brag about what we had. I *did* immediately think of us and of how lucky I was to have found you. But I would never purposely betray you with ridicule and disloyalty. I was trying to tell that cop, 'You may have thought you wanted one kind of existence until your destiny made itself known. Go with it. It's who you really are.' I was giddy, for him and for us. It's why I posted and never went back. I didn't think I was saying anything bad. I thought I was dropping joy all over the place. As I said, *fucking Internet.*"

Charlie, too, thought *fucking Internet*. It was too literal and not clear enough. It was black and white and too dangerous for the gray of life. It kept people plugged in but disconnected. It was a peculiar universe that had no business asserting jurisdiction over anyone's relationship.

And yet, as it could be foe, so, too, was it friend. Charlie and Bryce still hadn't told their family or friends about their breakup, and they had gotten away with it because of technology.

Charlie knew they were just about to be uncovered and that they had pushed it to the outer limits, but for eight weeks—which was brief in technology time since one post could tide over people for a week or longer—they had been able to put up a front and stave off the shame of rejection they each had endured. They had used the very thing that had hurt them most to save face. It had been an odyssey.

Ultimately, Charlie relished the world outside and the words Bryce spoke to him then, in their living room.

"I wish I could make sense to you," Charlie said, "about what you mean to me, standing here, in the real world. All I can say is I'm sorry. For everything. You were right that I failed and should have had more trust."

"I torched it."

"After I poured the gasoline and ruined us." It felt great to say it. Charlie wanted them to say it all, to leave nothing unsaid, as they had done, because of his poor choices, on the night he had left.

"I violated our intimate world and betrayed our privacy," Bryce said.

"And I overreacted to an absurd degree."

Charlie glanced at the Helsinki photo again. It wasn't just a perfect picture. It was a picture-perfect reflection of how well they had harmonized for seven years. Charlie swore right then they would have that again.

"I'm embarrassed," Charlie said. "*I should have had more faith.* That's what faith is. Understanding what can't be understood, what makes no sense. *Trusting* the source of the pain to have an explanation for hurting you, when it's the love of your life who appears guilty. *This* is the conversation we should have had. *That day.* These are the words you may have said if you weren't blindsided and in the fight of your life. No matter how tortured I was with humiliation, I should have considered you and remembered you would never hurt me on purpose."

Bryce interrupted him with several kisses. "Babe."

"I'm so sorry for what I did to us," Charlie said, "and for all those horrible things I said the day I left. I've had nightmares about it. I wish I had behaved better. I felt cast away, and I returned the favor and deserted you instead of asking you to throw me a life preserver. What we have, what you have inside you, could have kept me afloat. But I swam away to other shores."

He rubbed his hands along Bryce's back. His tone was comforting, private, affectionate. "You've been carrying a full load of guilt, when at least half should have been pushed back on me." He spoke even softer. "You tried to tell me at my apartment that I was guilty too, and I wouldn't listen. You practically banged your head against the wall to get me to see reason and to act like a partner, *your* partner. I'm sorry I didn't stay and fight through it."

"I love you almost more than I can withstand right now," Bryce said.

Their kisses were ferocious and hungry and compensating.

When they came up for air, Charlie asked the one thing he had to know. "Can you forgive me? Do you believe I will never again lose faith? Please tell me that the water will flow again."

"The water is flowing, Charlie. We're in full bloom. I don't think we ever dried up or died. I know we didn't. I love you. I always will. And I trust you. Completely. I know I pushed you to leave. You never would have done it, otherwise. I'm too guilty myself to withhold forgiveness, but even if I weren't, I would still forgive you. It's that faith you talked about. The person you are, Charlie, would never do something I couldn't forgive. I just hope you can forgive me."

"I already did. I think before I rang the doorbell. Maybe even before the movie theater. But especially after hearing what you said about the way we met and what I meant to you. I know you got tripped up, by words on a screen. I know you aren't capable, either, of doing something I couldn't forgive."

"Babe, Babe, Babe. God, I love you." Words and kisses blended.

"I love you, too. More than I have any other day in my life. And I'll prove it with the ultimate sacrifice. I'll leave Culver City for you."

They laughed, as best friends and lovers and partners.

They lay on the couch all night, as the longest prelude ever to lovemaking, and, after sunrise on Friday and a shared hot shower, went to bed, where, in the broad daylight of their sanctuary, Charlie made love to Bryce with a blatant lack of inhibition. He gave himself unreservedly, generously, liberally, and with no concerns about what he had read two months before. It was the freest he had been in seven years because he had been given something he hadn't needed before but was happy to have then. He had a special reassurance that Bryce had chosen him because he was Charlie and that what he offered was the only thing Bryce desired. He showed it off, he shared and bared it all, he strutted.

And he realized nothing was different from Bryce's end and that the answer was there all the time. If he had had more faith, he would have seen it. Bryce gave himself to Charlie with the same abandon he always had, with the same looks of love and pleasure and thrill on his face he had always shown when they made love.

Before Charlie left two months earlier, he had always thought the world disappeared for Bryce when they were together. Everything but Charlie seemed to fall away, almost as though Bryce were enchanted by a spell. In Culver City, Charlie had been plagued with the notion that it had been Bryce's way of coping with not finding Charlie attractive. He thought maybe Bryce had "checked out" when they made love and taken himself someplace else. But Charlie saw the same bearing and expressions that Friday morning and knew it had nothing to do with "hanging in there". Bryce was so completely drawn in by Charlie, by their lovemaking, that he was unmoored from the rest of life. Charlie had wanted to be all of that for Bryce. What he knew that Friday was that, when they made love, he was simply all. He was all Bryce wanted or needed. It drew Charlie even closer than he already was. He had never been in love or made love as deeply and completely as he was and did that day. It was all-encompassing and threatened to enthrall them for days and days and days.

When it was over, technology reappeared. They found online a group that performed wedding ceremonies at a moment's notice. The click-and-find wedding planners offered beach, rooftop, faux-chapel, and other settings and even took care of the marriage license hassles, at the drop.

Charlie and Bryce booked a beach wedding for 8:18 a.m. the next day, Saturday, and used that day, a very different kind of Friday from the one eight weeks earlier, to text, e-mail, and post online invitations to the wedding, with calls to close family members delivering the good news. Charlie's mom had said it had been about time.

They asked for no gifts and assured people the ceremony would be short. They knew they gave people no notice. And, anyway, they had something to take care of Saturday afternoon, which they didn't want anyone to find out about, least of all their families.

Texts, e-mails, and online RSVPs flooded in. Most people they invited would be at the wedding. Charlie marveled again at what a bizarre accomplice technology had made. It allowed them to plan a wedding over the course of just twelve hours and invite their loved ones with a few clicks—and shop for rings while they waited for RSVPs. It was astounding to realize it had also almost ruined their lives. It all reminded Charlie of cars, which could kill a person or get them to the hospital in an emergency and save their life.

——◆——

The wedding was perfect. Spontaneous games of beach volleyball and Frisbee broke out, and people stayed even after Charlie and Bryce finally left.

They had used healthy amounts of their vacation time during the Culver City Era and agreed they would honeymoon in Helsinki in November when they had more time saved. And they would still throw a house-buying bash, three years from then, for all the people who were too far away to attend their beach nuptials.

After the wedding, that same Saturday, they ran that errand they didn't want anyone to know about. They moved Charlie's things out of Culver City. Charlie gave Grayson his keys and forfeited his deposit. As Bryce had guessed, Grayson never batted an eye and even congratulated them on their newlywed status. He had had no real interest in Charlie. Charlie hadn't cared either way, but he found Bryce's perfect assessment uncanny. It gave him that much more faith in all the other things Bryce had said about him.

They had needed to take a taxi there so Bryce could drive Charlie's car and Charlie could ride his motorcycle home. But the Culver City Era had ended.

After Charlie unpacked, they drove to Goodwill and donated the two large suitcases. They wanted no remnants of Culver City in Santa Monica. It meant spending the late afternoon which would soon become their wedding night at the loading dock of a thrift store, but they figured that's what married best friends were for.

They spent Saturday night, their wedding night, in bed, insisting that the best part of their honeymoon not wait until Helsinki in November, and continued the celebration on Sunday on their couch. It wasn't football season, and, for once, they were glad. They had other things to do and so much they had missed to share, about Japan, about phone calls, about longings. It was their first full day back together with no major distractions.

They each slid into work on Monday and talked baseball. And weddings.

They posted pictures of the ceremony and texted each other all week at work, giddy, in love, and feeling reminiscent of their first week together.

They accepted that technology would always be a factor in their lives, but they resolved to use it wisely and to never rely on it primarily, to always let each other explain anything in real life that didn't make sense online, and to turn it all off for no reason at all as often as they could get away with it. And they replaced their home computer, to remove painful reminders.

After they were married, Bryce still stood and sat and lay and slept too close, and lightly stroked Charlie's feet while he read a book in their bed, and it had finally dawned on Charlie that Bryce did so because he was deeply attached to Charlie, and the nearness comforted him.

Charlie then had an epiphany. He had been guilty for seven years of his own childish notion. Because Bryce was beautiful, Charlie assumed he was confident, if not in all things, certainly in his relationship with Charlie. Charlie realized he sometimes didn't work hard enough to reassure Bryce because he figured it was unnecessary and might even make him appear idiotic—only a tomfool would reassure Adonis. Bryce had always had to reach for Charlie who proved elusive in the end without meaning to. Bryce had tried to tell Charlie the day he left that even when Charlie was near, he felt far away and that Bryce had wanted to hold onto him always. It was that swagger Bryce had said Charlie had that made him seem hard to pin down, even as he planned to go nowhere, except Charlie had made Bryce's most dreaded fear come true and had left without warning.

Charlie righted those wrongs. After the Culver City Era, it was Charlie who sometimes stood or sat or lay or slept too close. And stroked Bryce's feet while he read in their bed. He made sure Bryce knew he would never leave, no matter what they faced. He couldn't. He loved Bryce. Bryce loved him. And for each other, they were all of that.

About the Author

Sailor Penniman lives in Los Angeles and writes modern literature short stories and novellas. Sailor enjoys featuring Los Angeles in a story's narrative, wherever possible, and using the city's diverse palette of life circumstances to weave tales of love, perseverance, and equality.

@sailorpenniman